NO AMENDS

BY
ANGELA LAM

Publisher: Gross Productions
Cover Designer: RL Design
Editor: Jovana Shirley

Print ISBN: 979-8-9857935-2-9

For Doug.
Liars are the best storytellers.

Also by Angela Lam

Novels:

Legs

Out of Balance

Blood Moon Rising

The Divorce Planner

Friends First

The Women of the Crush Series

Short Stories:

The Human Act and Other Stories

Memoirs:

Red Eggs and Good Luck

The Fool and the Magician

Chapter One

TANG
Present Day
Bodega Bay, California

"Sorry I'm late," Layla whispered, crawling into bed.

Tang rolled toward her, pulled by the force of the weight on the mattress. A sliver of moonlight from the space where the curtains failed to meet illuminated Layla's broad silhouette. Even though the Pacific Ocean was several hundred yards away, its sound filled the room like a third person snoring.

Tang blinked several times and yawned. "How was your trip?"

She had known Layla was supposed to return home sometime tonight after spending the weekend with her brother on the East Coast to settle their mother's estate. But nothing had gone as planned this weekend, so Layla's delay wasn't surprising.

"There was an accident on the highway at Hangman's Bend. Someone went over the cliff."

A chill crept over Tang's body and stiffened her limbs when Layla mentioned the nickname locals gave to the sharp turn in the road overlooking the Pacific Ocean. "Did you see the vehicle?"

"No. Just smoke from the flames." Layla snuggled close and kissed her shoulder.

Tang shuddered against the warm intimacy. *Dee.* Guilt dug into her side. She rolled over, away from Layla, suddenly queasy. *Maybe it wasn't Dee.* She wrapped her arms around her waist and closed her eyes, replaying the fight.

A funny feeling niggled in the pit of her stomach, and she searched Dee's purse when she was in the bathroom. The New

1

York State–issued driver's license was registered to Deidre James, not Dee Young.

Hurt and betrayal blurred Tang's vision. *"What else don't I know?"*

Tang shoved the memories into a corner of her mind and tried to breathe through the pain. *Don't worry. The accident could have involved anyone.*

***

As usual, Tang woke before Layla, brewed a pot of coffee, and carried a steaming mug into the sunroom. Fog blanketed the view outside the windows. The room felt cold and damp for summer. Tang turned on a light beside her writing desk. She hadn't finished her manuscript over the weekend, as promised. But Tang couldn't focus. Not even after a second cup of coffee, sweetened with vanilla creamer.

Who was in the accident early this morning?

She carried the laptop to the sofa and curled up in a pillowed corner, tucking her feet under her hips. She typed *Highway 1 auto accident* in the search bar and scanned the first page of results. With trembling fingers, she clicked on the top entry—*Fatal Crash Reported Off Bodega Bay Cliff.*

Posted at 5:48 a.m., August 7th

A pickup truck plunged down a cliff off Highway 1 near Bodega Bay early Monday morning, according to the California Highway Patrol. A fire was reported at 12:12 a.m. near the Salmon Creek Ranger Station. Firefighters found the driver dead inside the burning vehicle. More information will be released as it becomes available.

Tang closed the tab and shut down the computer. *There are tons of pickups in Sonoma County.* She set the laptop on the coffee table beside the empty mug and uncurled from her perch on the sofa. *The driver could have been anyone.*

On wobbly legs, she padded down the dark hallway to the kitchen and grabbed her cell phone off the charger on the counter, where she left it each night before going to bed. She tapped the Call Settings under Contacts and unblocked a phone number before sending a text.

—*Are you OK?*—

She pressed Send and waited, staring at the screen. Hope beat like anxious bird wings in her throat. Minutes later, the message still showed *Delivered*. A cold chill settled deep in her bones. She shoved the phone into a warm pocket of her robe and paced along the hardwood floor. The weak spots in the planks groaned beneath her slippers.

A list of logical reasons marched through her mind. *Maybe she turned off her phone. Maybe she forgot to charge her battery. Maybe she already boarded a plane back to New York. Maybe, maybe, maybe ...*

Pausing by the kitchen sink, she checked the phone one more time—*Delivered*. Sighing, she returned the phone to a pocket and braced her hands against the cool counter. She gazed at the fog dispersing along the coastline. Even through the dual-paned window, the waves roared and rumbled. Fear and anxiety powered through her.

What to do? What to do? The question, a mantra.

Blinking rapidly, she stepped back, dropped her arms to the sides, and breathed in and out as slowly and as deeply as she had been trained years ago to do during a season of panic attacks. As soon as the danger passed, she picked up a pen and scribbled on a notepad.

Went for a run on the beach. Be back soon. XOXO.

She kept her workout gear in the spare bedroom, never wanting to wake up the late-sleeping Layla. With fumbling fingers, she dressed quickly and slipped out the back door, taking the worn steps carefully down to the beach, the sharp wind biting into her cheeks and the guttural sound of the waves crashing in her ears.

Chapter Two

DEE
Four Days Ago
Upper West Side, New York City, New York

"Mommy's home!"

As soon as I wheeled my luggage into the apartment but before I shut the door, Tyler ran into my body. A crash of arms and legs tangled around me from waist to ankle. I laughed, tossing aside my purse, my keys jangling to the linoleum floor. Half–bending over, half-kneeling, I stroked his still-chubby cheek, kissed the top of his towhead, and rubbed beneath his smooth eight-year-old chin.

"Hey, sunshine," Ryan said, emerging from the galley kitchen. "How was Chicago?"

"Same as always."

I disentangled from Tyler and strode into my husband's embrace. He smelled of garlic and lemon from the dinner he was cooking, and his kiss was divine, just enough to hint at what would come later, after Tyler was tucked into bed.

I picked up my purse and keys and placed them on the side table, kicked off my heels, and slung my jacket over the crook of my arm. With my free hand, I tugged the suitcase past the living room, where Tyler watched TV, and closed the door to the master bedroom, where I undressed, dumping the clothes I had worn on the flight back from the Windy City and those packed in the suitcase into the hamper.

Next, a quick, hot shower, followed by a new set of clothes—one of Ryan's worn T-shirts and a pair of yoga pants, bare feet. After padding into the living room, I rummaged through my purse for my phone, then sank into the sofa, stretching out my legs on the coffee table beside Tyler's sketchpad. My toenail polish was chipped. I would have to get them done tomorrow, if the spa could fit me in on such short notice. But right now, I didn't worry. I was home. Ryan was cooking. Tyler was drawing a monster truck.

I scrolled through messages. One from Chris, asking when my flight would arrive in San Francisco on Saturday. I sighed, not wanting to engage with my twin brother at the moment, and selected the next text from Veronica, a server I had met during a layover in Utah.

I smiled. *Ah, she misses me.*

Emojis of hugs and kisses filled the text. I typed an equal number of hugs and kisses back, then moved on to Zoe, that nymph in Florida who could not follow directions. Frowning, I deleted her text—a picture of her new silicone breasts—and blocked her number. Next was a message from Hardy, a sweet guy I'd met at a coffee shop in Midtown who seemed too innocent to meddle with. But I could not resist temptation. He would buy the most expensive dinners because I had warned him to never buy me a gift. Sex was mediocre, but the cuddling afterward was amazing.

Whenever we were apart, he sent such bland texts: *How was your day? Are you happy?*

I always felt obligated to respond: *My day was fine. I'm happy now that I've heard from you.*

The rest of the messages were from work, which I could respond to tomorrow. I sent a brief text to Aaron, confirming my appointment on Sunday to look at houses in Bodega Bay, then scrolled through, making sure I hadn't missed anything from *her*— Tang, my writer friend, my lover by the sea. Nothing. She never explained why she had stopped taking my calls months ago. But I could assume the reason was Layla, her live-in girlfriend, who worked with dirt, like a tomboy who never grew up.

I crossed my ankles and turned my phone facedown on my lap. I was a better catch than Layla. Why? As a salesperson, I had been trained to listen. My lovers had someone ready and willing to carry their burdens in exchange for anything I wanted—mostly time, sex, meals, and conversations. My lovers only received the best of me. Who wouldn't want that arrangement? Apparently, not Tang, who believed I was single and lonely, tied down by two aging parents. But I knew I could change her mind. Because love was like business. Sometimes, you needed to be present, in person, to get the deal done.

"Dinner in five minutes." Ryan poked his head around the corner, smiling, his blue eyes shining.

"Okay, sweetheart." I turned my phone faceup and circled back to my brother, my finger hovering over the keypad.

If the plane left JFK at eight, as scheduled, I would arrive in SFO at eleven. Oh, what the heck? I decided to forward my itinerary instead.

—I'll take a cab if you're at work.—

Moments later, I received a response.

—No problem. I'll pick you up.—

"Dinner's ready." Ryan carried out the dishes to set the table in the dining room.

He was a good father and a good husband. He deserved someone devoted to him completely, but he had chosen me, someone who was always looking for someone else.

"Hurry up, chicken butt," I said, ruffling the back of Tyler's head. "Last one to the table does dishes."

"Ah, Mom, you're no fun."

"I thought you missed me." I pouted.

Tyler turned off the TV, closed his notebook, and stood, reaching for my hand. "I miss you because I love you." When he smiled, he looked just like me—blond hair, dark brown eyes, and red lips.

"I love you too." I let him lead me into the bathroom, where we took turns washing our hands.

The smells of halibut and wild rice and steamed root vegetables filled the apartment.

My stomach grumbled.

Oh, how good it was to be home.

I turned off my phone and pulled back a chair, sitting between Tyler and Ryan.

"Are you picking out our vacation home this weekend?" Ryan asked.

6

I shrugged, wondering how much longer I could play this charade. "I've narrowed the choices to three properties along the Sonoma Coast. I promise to send pictures."

Ryan cut into his halibut. "Ty and I can fly out next weekend to join you."

"Sure, that would be wonderful." I flashed a smile at Tyler. "You can show Uncle Chris the book you made at the community center."

Tyler grumbled, pushing his rice back and forth across the plate. "I don't want to make him upset."

"Oh, sweetheart, you'd just be sharing what you made."

But even I knew Chris would take the printed booklet and think, *He's a real writer and not me.*

"Hey, hey, hey." Ryan wagged his fork. "Don't be picking on Uncle Chris. He does a lot for us, especially letting you stay at his home so you can pocket your expense money. That's the only way we'd be able to afford the down payment on that vacation home."

Of course, Ryan thought in terms of dollars and cents. He was a corporate accountant. I took a sip of lukewarm water. I sure did miss the iced spa water at the hotel. Tomorrow, I'd have to pick up cucumbers and watermelon on the way back from getting my nails done.

"How have things been at home?"

I listened to Tyler jabber about the new friends he had made at the community center and Ryan talk about the changes at work. A warmth spread throughout my body, filling me with peace and contentment.

I loved my family.

But I loved Tang just a little bit more.

Chapter Three

TANG
Fourteen Months Ago
San Francisco, California

Tang pushed away from the revolving glass doors of the Mark Hopkins hotel and scuttled around the idling cars in the stone driveway to the empty sidewalk. Whoever said the coldest winter was a summer in San Francisco had been right. The brisk wind billowed up her skirt, and she hugged her peacoat tighter, increasing her pace up the sloped street. She didn't know where she was headed. She only knew she wanted to get away as quickly as possible.

Frustration bristled up her spine. How could she tell Layla the conference had been a waste of money? Bile soured her mouth. She had been so close to finding representation. Three literary agents had loved her concept of a romantic comedy in which the two main characters found each other through the intercession of their dead parents, but all three of them had wanted her to change the setting and make the couple interracial.

"No one wants *Crazy Rich Asians* with ghosts. We need American diversity," one of the literary agents had said. "Then, we can ask for a five-hundred-thousand-dollar advance *and* sell movie rights."

Defeat slumped against her shoulders. No one wanted the story she had written about two wealthy Asians living overseas, who found each other through their ancestors. Worse, the agents she had spoken with all wanted a story she knew in her heart she could not write.

Tugging the coat tighter, she plodded up the steep street. Pain shot through her tight calves. Oh, why hadn't she packed sneakers? Because she had planned to dine at Top of the Mark with other aspiring writers, watching the sun set over the Golden Gate

8

Bridge and toasting to success. Humiliation and labored breathing squeezed from her chest.

At the end of the street, she paused mid-stride, captivated by the fairy-tale glow of candlelight in the floor-to-ceiling windows of a corner restaurant. The past three days and two nights, she had dined with nosy strangers who wanted to know what she was writing. Tonight, she would eat alone, away from failure. She pushed open the door and stepped inside the enveloping warmth and comforting scents of grilled seafood, cocktail sauce, and sweet wine.

"Table for two?" the host asked.

She scanned the intimate tables, draped in white cloth and sparkling silverware and candlelight. Too bad Layla was nestled in their cozy kitchen in Bodega Bay and not here with her.

She blinked back the welling emotion and nodded toward the bar at the back of the restaurant. "Just one."

Chapter Four

DEE
Fourteen Months Ago
San Francisco, California

I sat at the bar, glancing out the full-length window, waiting for my brother, Chris, who was always late.

The middle-aged woman slipped onto the barstool next to me, away from the men in business suits, hunched side by side, nursing drinks or chatting on phones.

The bartender, a wiry man with circular glasses, wiped down the space in front of her. "What can I get you?"

She hung her purse beneath the counter and shrugged off her coat, folding it once before laying it across her lap. "I'll have a Hemingway."

I wrinkled my nose. Another writer. Like my brother.

"Coming right up." He winked.

She didn't respond to his flirting. She was a stone wall.

I snuck a second look. Sleek pageboy bob, exotic eyes, petite legs to match her short stature. She was a cute china doll, delicate and unique. I wanted to take her to my hotel room and play with her.

I swiveled, my ponytail almost brushing her arm. "You're a writer." I smiled, all red lips and squinty eyes. "What are you writing?"

The woman flinched, as if my words had singed her like hot coals. "How do you know I'm a writer?" She cocked her head to the side and narrowed her gaze.

She was a suspicious woman by nature. I would have to work extra hard to gain her trust.

"Lucky guess." I swirled the straw in my Long Island iced tea. "My brother's a writer too. Unpublished. Been writing for all eternity, it seems. I don't think he'll ever make it, but don't tell him I said that." I placed a finger over my lips. "Whenever we have drinks, he orders a Hemingway. 'For inspiration.' " I made air quotes with my fingers before glancing at the door.

"Ah, he's here." I stood and greeted the tall, lanky man with a kiss on the cheek and a long hug. "Ready?"

He motioned to the woman I had been chatting up. "Introduce me to your friend."

The woman smiled and held out her hand. "Tang Young."

Laughing, Chris shook her hand. "What a coincidence. We're also Youngs. Dee and Christopher." He waved a broad hand between us, always forgetting I had changed my name when I married years ago. "You from here?"

"Bodega Bay, about two hours north."

"Ah, yes, that little fishing town where Alfred Hitchcock chose to film *The Birds*." He sat on the other side of her and leaned across the counter to catch my gaze. "Remember that movie, Dee?"

"Ugh." I shuddered. "I had nightmares for weeks."

Chris nodded at Tang's almost-empty glass. "I see you have good taste."

I leaned across the bar. "Tang's a writer too."

"Ah, you are?" Chris shifted his position to examine her more closely.

Tang dipped her head toward her chest. "I'd rather not talk about writing."

"Of course." Chris nodded, and the wave of brown hair bobbed against his forehead. "A writer never discusses a work in progress. It dilutes the story's power." He waved to the bartender. "Two Hemingways. One for me and one for the young lady." He glanced over the top of her head. "What are you having, sis?"

"I'm good." I sipped through the straw in my cocktail. "I'm saving myself for dinner."

He chuckled. "Women … always on a diet, right?" He nudged Tang's shoulder.

"Right." The word escaped from her mouth like a knee-jerk reaction. Just like the heat invading her cheeks. Anyone could see she hadn't come here to get picked up by a man she had just met.

Especially not another writer. "Thank you, but I can buy my own drinks." The awkwardness of the situation weighed on her. She opened her purse and tossed a few bills on the counter.

"Wait." He placed his hand on her wrist. "I'm sorry if I offended you." Worry lines creased his forehead. "I just thought I was being friendly."

Yeah, right. Chris was always saying the wrong thing when it came to women. I didn't always intervene, but I liked this woman.

"Leave her alone, Chris. She's taken."

"Dee's right." Tang stood and shoved her arms into her peacoat. She glanced in my direction. "Lucky guess?"

Smoldering with confidence, I tilted my chin, exposing the long length of my bare neck—the neck I knew she wanted to kiss. A slow smile spread across my face. "The luckiest."

She widened her gaze and rubbed the tips of her fingers together.

Oh, yes. I'd hit the jackpot. I recognized that look. That spark of inspiration.

Without saying good-bye, she spun on her heels, wove around the maze of tables, and tumbled into the open arms of the night.

I turned toward Chris. "Now, are you ready?"

He gaped. "What did I do wrong?"

I laughed, touching his arm. "Everything. And nothing." Standing, I linked my arm through his. "Let her go."

My brother was innocent. He played for keeps. I played to keep the other party guessing. How much did I love them? How many plans could we set up? How many years could my other life go undetected? How many hearts could I break and mend and break again?

I smiled, knowing the most important answer. "She's mine."

Chapter Five

TANG
Fourteen Months Ago
San Francisco, California

At breakfast, Tang carried her tray of scrambled eggs and toast to the table where the three literary agents sat. "May I join you?" She hovered beside them, waiting.

Ken Carson with Literary Excellence glanced over his shoulder. He arched a silver eyebrow, his dark eyes gleaming. "Why, yes, you may."

She set down the tray and pulled back the chair, her pulse thumping wildly in her palms. From the instructions given at the start of the conference, she knew she couldn't pitch her new idea without an invitation, but she wasn't worried. A newfound confidence thrummed through her.

"Thanks." She sipped her coffee and smiled. "I was up way too late, rewriting my synopsis and sample chapters based on all the great feedback I'd received."

Melissa Minder with Top-Notch Literary pointed her fork at the table. "Aren't you the one with the ghost story?"

"I tweaked the concept." Tang held the buttered toast over her plate. "The main characters who get together are no longer living in Singapore, but they're here, in San Francisco. One works for the Federal Reserve Bank; the other helps her parents in a tourist shop in Chinatown. One is a white man who believes in the power of independence and freedom; the other is a Chinese American woman who clings to the hope of fate and destiny. When they meet, their ideas and cultures clash, and it's only through the intercession of their dead parents that they are finally united before living their happily ever after."

Ken chewed thoughtfully, then swallowed, rinsing his mouth with a sip of water. "I like it." He shifted his body toward her. "Do you mind sending me those new pages?" He handed her his business card. "Type *SFWC* in the subject line."

"Thank you." The card felt like a golden ticket in her warm hand. "I will."

By the time the first break ended that morning, she had emailed the new synopsis and sample chapters to Ken, and he had responded. She sat in her hotel room, rereading the email several times before checking out of her room and wheeling her suitcase to the front desk for them to store until the conference ended.

Strands of his words scrolled like movie credits against the big screen of her mind—*brilliant concept, happy to extend representation, will send over the contract early next week, can't wait to chat by phone to develop the novel for submission, already have three publishers in mind.*

The offer made her buoyant, and she typed a quick text to Layla.

—I did it. I have a literary agent.—

She didn't mention the full rewrite or how long before the novel would hit publishers' inboxes because she didn't want any questions she couldn't answer or any of Layla's hard-nosed comments puncturing the delicate soap bubble of hope that floated inside of her. She waited at the bank of elevators, ready to head up to the third floor for the final hours of the conference, when she noticed Dee striding across the lobby.

Chapter Six

DEE
Fourteen Months Ago
San Francisco, California

"Dee!"

I spun in the direction of my name and smiled when I placed the face with the voice. "Tang, good to see you again."

She rushed across the lobby, her face flushed with happiness. "I need to thank you for inspiring me."

I tossed back my blonde ponytail and chuckled. "Why aren't you thanking that Hemingway you ordered?"

Tang clutched her hands—a supplicant. "Because when you said you were the luckiest, that phrase triggered a whole new concept for my novel that had been previously rejected by three literary agents." The words gushed like water flowing downstream. "I stayed up and rewrote the sample chapters and synopsis. This morning, I received an offer for representation." She bounced on the balls of her feet, the smile straining her cheeks. "Thank you."

"We need to celebrate." I touched her elbow—a subtle gesture. "I know just the place to go for a midday drink."

Tang glanced over her shoulder at the bank of elevators. "I still have three hours left of the writers' conference."

"Then, we can meet in the lobby at three o'clock. I'm staying here since my brother got lucky last night too." I tilted my head and widened my smile. "Seems like I'm every writer's muse."

Disappointment sagged against Tang's shoulders. "I can't. Layla's picking me up then. She doesn't like to linger."

Last night, when I had told Chris she was taken, I didn't know I had spoken the truth.

I shook my head, pretending I didn't have that problem and offered up a solution instead. "Well … do you have to stay for the rest of the sessions? Or can you play hooky?"

She stood, mesmerized. Finally, she decided. "No, I can leave."

Smiling, I linked my arm through hers and spun toward the revolving doors. "Let's go."

Chapter Seven

TANG
Fourteen Months Ago
San Francisco, California

Cool sunlight glinted off the hoods of parked cars against the sloped street. Tang thought she heard her cell phone ping, and she slipped her arm out of the crook of Dee's elbow and rustled around her purse. Squinting, she swiped her finger across the screen. Her heartbeat thumped in her chest, and her fingers trembled. No messages.

Why hadn't Layla responded to her good news?

"Something wrong?" Dee scooted closer, bending her head and pointing.

Sighing, Tang tossed the phone into her purse. "Everything's fine."

Layla was probably in another room and hadn't heard the text. Maybe she should call her. Or just wait to deliver the news in person.

"You don't look fine." Dee placed a hand on Tang's back.

The warmth penetrated through to her skin. Tang swiveled, witnessing the concern on Dee's pinched face. *She cares*. Her resistance softened. *Maybe she'll understand.*

"I was just hoping Layla would respond to my good news."

"I wouldn't worry about it." Dee nudged her toward the café and held open the glass door, waving her inside. "You two have all the time in the world together. All we have is right now."

Nodding, Tang slipped into the cozy warmth and lively chatter of Sunday patrons nestled shoulder to shoulder in tight booths. The air was heavy with the scent of bacon and eggs.

A host seated them at a booth in the back.

When the server arrived a moment later, Dee smiled and waved away the menus. "We'll have two mimosas, hold the orange juice." Shifting her attention back to Tang, she smiled. "How exciting! You have a literary agent. Chris would be so jealous." She narrowed her eyes into black slits and laughed.

Tang remembered the dazed look of confusion on Christopher's face when she'd rejected his offer to buy her a drink last night. The sting of her words had felt like a slap, and she wondered, "Did I hurt his feelings last night?"

"Don't worry about him." Dee smirked and flicked her wrist. "He's a straight guy in San Francisco. He thinks *every* woman is interested. I'm from New York. I assume no woman is interested."

Tang tilted her head, considering the statement. "I'm interested." The words felt fragile, leaving her mouth. She almost wished she could take them back.

"You are?" Dee lifted her chin, and the blonde ponytail slid over her shoulder and dangled across her chest. A slow smile rose like sunrise, brightening her features. She wove her fingers through Tang's hand and squeezed. "I wouldn't be here if I wasn't interested."

Excitement heated Tang's cheeks. She glanced at Dee's fingers, her own hand a foreign object, and listened to the thunder crashing against her ribs.

The server delivered their drinks.

Dee withdrew her hand and grasped the flute of champagne. "To your literary agent."

Tang lifted her glass. "To your inspiration."

She clicked the edge of her glass and took a sip. The fizzy fluid buzzed against her tongue and floated down her throat, warming her insides. She twirled the stem of the glass against the table, her gaze downcast. Guilt bubbled up, threatening to extinguish her happiness. *Why am I here, celebrating my success with another woman, when I should be back at the conference, listening to more experienced writers share their knowledge?*

She shoved the thought aside and lifted her head. "What do you do in New York?"

Dee smiled. "I'm a sales rep for a tech start-up. Our innovative software helps consumers build their credit. Our target audience began with college students. But lately, we've shifted our focus to expand our market. Now, we embrace those recovering from job losses, outstanding medical bills, and bankruptcy." She took a sip of champagne. "As a result, my territory has grown from the East Coast to nationwide." She steadied her gaze. "I'm in the Bay Area at least once a month. I always manage to extend my stay to include a visit with my brother … and now, hopefully, with you."

The invitation swept across Tang's vast imagination. What about Layla? The future unfurled before her, dark and dangerous and unknown. She tapped her fingers against the scarred wooden table, playing for time, hoping for her phone to ping with a message, reassuring her everything was all right when nothing was and never would be again.

With one nervous gulp, she swallowed the rest of the champagne and set aside the empty glass. Reaching across the table, she brushed her fingertips across Dee's wrist. "I live with my girlfriend in Bodega Bay, an hour-and-a-half drive north of San Francisco. She's a geotech engineer with the county, and I sell real estate when I'm not writing. If you want to visit, you'll have to visit both of us as friends."

For a long moment, Dee held the tension in a silent gaze. Then, with one swift motion, she leaned across the table and grazed Tang's lips with a kiss.

The unexpected touch lit up a maze of desire. Tang lifted her hips off the bench seat, her mouth eager as she surrendered to that forbidden feeling, parting her lips and slipping her tongue into the warm, moist cavern of Dee's mouth.

Moments later, when the kiss ended, Tang slumped against the hard back of the banquette and gasped. She had never felt so fully seen, known, and loved. Not by Layla. Not by her parents. Not by anyone. Until now. With Dee. Her muse and her desire. Her whole being swelled with happiness and fulfillment.

"I don't think I can be just friends with someone who kisses as good as you do." Dee removed her wallet from her purse and set a twenty on the table. Standing, she crooked her finger.

19

As if in a trance, Tang followed. Outside, the wind blew across her face like a reprimand. Guilt and fear crowded into the pit of her stomach.

"We don't have to kiss." The lie burned her tongue.

For a long moment, Dee held her gaze. Dark desire filled her dilating pupils. "Oh, yes, we do."

Tang closed her eyes, feeling Dee's lips against her mouth, her tongue teasing out doubt. *Oh, Layla, I'm sorry*. She wrapped her arms around Dee's neck, aligning their soft bodies together, sealing herself away from whatever thoughts and feelings threatened to extinguish the delightful sensation of being seen and chosen and wanted more than anything else in the world.

Chapter Eight

DEE
Two Days Ago
San Francisco, California

"May I borrow the truck tomorrow?"

"Sure." Chris drove from the airport to his apartment, located in a high-rise near Lake Merced.

The fog burned off the ocean, leaving a trail of white streaks like ribbons of mist through the atmosphere.

I checked my makeup in the visor mirror, then scrolled through my messages. Damn. In my haste to leave the city, I'd forgotten to pack the book I was reading to Tyler.

"Can we stop at the bookstore?"

He grumbled, turning off the highway and taking the road to Stonestown Galleria. "I don't like shopping at the big-box stores."

"I know." I patted his arm. "But I forgot the mystery I'm reading to Tyler. He expects a chapter each night."

"What if they don't have a copy?" He shot a sidelong glance.

I shrugged. "It's a mainstream book. I'm sure they'll have it."

"Aren't you Miss Confidence?"

I narrowed my gaze. "You're normally not this moody. What's bugging you? Bad writing day?"

He sighed, turning into the parking lot, searching for an empty spot. He hunched his shoulders and grimaced. "I don't like what you're planning on doing."

"You're just jealous." I winked, knowing Chris hadn't slept with a woman in so long that he could claim celibacy.

He gripped the steering wheel so tightly that his knuckles glowed white. "It's not fair to anyone, especially Ryan."

I snickered. "Ryan's never home."

"*You're* never home." He swerved into a spot and turned off the engine. "You're always traveling."

"It's my job. I'm in sales. My territory is the continental United States." I huffed. "At least the company has another employee to send overseas."

"But if they didn't, you'd go, wouldn't you?" He released the seat belt.

"Of course I would." I grabbed my purse and opened the door. The cool air splashed over my body, and I relished the sensation after the heated argument with my brother—an argument I knew would never end.

"I think you're making a mistake."

I flicked my wrist. "You think *all* of my decisions are mistakes." Which was true.

He hadn't approved of my marrying Ryan or having Tyler. He thought I was selfish. Whatever I did outside the home stayed outside the home. I never brought a lover to my family's apartment, and I never let a lover know where I lived. Most of the time, I never even used my real name. I was safe, and so was my family.

"I don't know why you're complaining. Ryan and Tyler don't care. I always come home." I stalked across the parking lot and stepped inside the temperate store, heading toward the children's books in the center.

Chris strode beside me. Even from the corner of my eye, I could see his hands clenched into fists. He didn't have to understand my lifestyle, but he did have to respect me.

"It's not right," he said. "Someday, you'll regret not doing the right thing."

I ran my fingers along the spines of the titles and authors listed in the mystery section until I found the book I needed, the one I'd promised to finish reading to Tyler. I plucked it from the shelf and carried it to the registers at the front of the store. I didn't understand Chris's morbid fixation on my lifestyle. He was a writer who lacked imagination. How else could he not comprehend the easy cat-and-mouse nature of love?

After I paid, I stalked out of the building and breathed in the fresh air. Cool for summer. Warm for the coast. I stood beside the white truck, tapping my foot, waiting while Chris let other cars pass.

How could we be twins and yet so different? One of us was always thinking ahead of the game while the other hung back, critical and observing.

Chapter Nine

TANG
Present Day
Bodega Bay, California

Through the fog, Tang ran along the curve of the beach, her feet pounding against the packed sand, her lungs heavy with oxygen. Sweat stuck to her skin despite the layers of fabric designed to keep her cool and dry. Anxiety and worry stormed across her chest, broken only by jagged flashes of anger.

Who was Dee Young? And why had Tang fallen so completely in love with her?

Above the cliffs, Tang glimpsed the trail up to the Salmon Creek fire station. Hope and fear fluttered in her stomach. Jogging in place, she considered her options—wait until the next press release or see if someone she knew might have been at the crash. Nodding, she raced up the crooked path cut into the side of the earth. She panted, and her thighs ached almost as badly as her strained lungs. Halfway up the steep incline, she glanced up toward the seagrass waving in the brisk wind, then down through the peekaboo wisps of fog blanketing the gray waves and brown beach. After several more steps, she crested above the pavement.

Through the lingering haze, the red-and-white firehouse loomed like a glowing beacon. Tang punched her fists against the sides of her hips and searched the firefighters unloading the truck parked in the driveway. The chill whipped through her clothes, and she shuddered.

Through the sea of bright yellow uniforms, she spotted Bert. The local children called him Big Bear because he was built like a grizzly—tall and brown with massive shoulders. He was known for his tremendous strength. He could haul strangers from burning buildings with one arm. Tang wondered if he had pried the dead body from the vehicle earlier this morning. She shivered and

24

marched toward the firehouse. Bert had a softer side too. He was the one who had calmed the hysterical child who had trapped his leg between the slats of a dining room chair while another firefighter sawed through the wood to set the boy free.

This softness reassured Tang, and she hustled toward him, waving her arms overhead. "Bert!"

He paused and turned in the direction of her voice. Beneath the yellow hard hat, his face was a full moon of smudges and smiles.

"Tang, what are you doing here?" He swept her into his arms and squeezed with just the right amount of pressure.

"Just running." She smiled and relaxed against the warm hug.

The two had been friends since Layla had introduced them seven years ago. Once a week, they gathered in the dining room of Layla and Tang's home and played blackjack along with Robin Snow, a professor emeritus of creative writing at Sonoma State University.

"I'm sorry I couldn't join you." He released her and took a step back.

Sometimes, Bert ran along the beach with her, covering six or seven miles.

She danced on the balls of her feet. "Were you at the crash this morning?"

He bowed his head and removed the hard hat to scratch above an ear. "Everyone responded." A line pinched between his eyebrows. "Why?"

"Just curious." She hated being cagey, but she really didn't want him to know the truth.

He tossed back his head and chuckled. "Don't tell me you're writing another story."

Smiling, she stilled her body. "I haven't finished the one I'm working on." The reminder of the deadline niggled another set of worries. "Layla mentioned the auto accident early this morning after coming home from visiting her brother, and I was concerned—that's all. Might have been someone we knew."

Frowning, he cradled the hard hat with both hands. "The body hasn't been identified yet."

"Will you tell me when you know?" She searched his face.

"The coroner's office doesn't typically notify us." He stepped closer and shifted his weight, casting a shadow between them. "You'll need to wait for the authorities to release the news of who she was."

She. Compounding worries twisted her stomach. Bile lurched to the back of her throat. She coughed, trying to clear the bitter fluid.

"You okay?" He took a step closer.

Shaking her head, she took a step back. "Not really."

"Odds are the woman was a stranger."

She nodded, but the knot in her gut tightened. "Thanks for telling me." She turned and jogged back toward the path to the beach.

"Hey, I'll see you tomorrow night."

"Seven o'clock," she shouted over her shoulder.

She paused at the mouth of the staircase cut into the side of the cliff. After testing her footing, she took the first step, then another until her feet rested on the packed sand. From a zippered pocket, she removed her cell phone and glanced at the screen. *Delivered*. A sharp wind blew the last tendrils of fog over her face, hiding the hot tears streaming down her cheeks.

***

When Tang returned to the warm house, she found a note on the kitchen counter, left by Layla.

Sorry I missed you. Hope you had a good run. See you tonight for dinner.

No *x*'s and *o*'s. No initial. Nothing to indicate the note was from Layla other than the fact that it was in her handwriting. Tang folded the stiff paper and placed her keys and phone beside it before she showered and changed for the day. Over the past year, her relationship with Layla had slowly eroded, much like the sea wind lashing at the house's siding, stripping away the layers until the root of their suffering lay bare for the world to see. She couldn't blame Dee, could she?

"Why must we marry?" Layla asked, long before her mother had fallen ill and died. "Why can't you be happy with what we have?"

"I need security," Tang said, folding her arms across her chest.

If they were married, she reasoned, then she wouldn't lose Layla, like she had lost her birth parents and her adoptive parents and every other person she had ever loved.

Why hadn't Layla answered, Security is an inside job? *Why had she kept her mouth shut, ending the discussion, planting the roots of bitterness deep in the soil of their love?*

Now, Tang carried a fresh banana smoothie into the sunroom and tried to focus on the story inspired by Dee fourteen months ago, but the blinking cursor winked, teasing her to distraction, and she returned to the kitchen to retrieve Layla's note, her keys, and her phone. The text message still indicated *Delivered*, and the fear and anger in her belly moved to her chest, tightening like a fist.

Where are you, Dee? Why can't I reach you? The questions piled up like stones along a retaining wall, keeping the knowledge and certainty away.

As soon as she set the phone on the coffee table, it rang.

She jolted against the soft sofa cushions, her fingers fumbling to answer. "Hello?"

"Good morning, Tang. I haven't received an email yet. I'm just checking to see if your story will be ready to go on submission to publishers next week."

The pounding in her chest eased when she heard Ken's inquisitive voice. She felt she could be honest with him, as honest as she could be with Dee. "I'm working on the ending, but I'm a little preoccupied. A friend who actually helped with the book's concept has gone missing, and I'm finding it hard to finish."

"I'm sorry to hear that," Ken said. His voice dripped with concern.

"May I have an extension?" Tang shifted on the sofa cushions, tucking her feet under her hips. Through the windows, she could see the roiling clouds in the gray sky. She took a deep breath and held it for a second longer than usual, hoping for a positive answer.

"I don't want to risk waiting." He cleared his throat. "The editor that I feel is perfect for the book is going on vacation in two weeks, and I'd like to look at the final draft to make sure it's perfect before then."

"Okay." Tang exhaled, considering her options. "How about I get it to you next week at the latest?"

"One week. That's it. Or you can find someone else to represent you."

A spike of fear punctured the stress. *I can't lose this opportunity. But will one week be long enough?* She bit her lower lip. If Aaron continued to cover her business, then she would be free to find answers and finish writing that final chapter.

"Okay. I'll call you as soon as I'm done."

***

That night, when Layla came home from work, Tang had dinner and a cocktail ready—beef wellington, wild rice, green beans, and a martini. She had set the table in the formal dining room instead of eating while standing around the stovetop, watching the TV news, like they usually did. She wanted to make Layla feel special. She wanted to make Layla feel loved. She wanted to make something in her life right.

"What's this?" Layla waved to the white tablecloth and folded cloth napkins, the fine china and silverware. Even tapered candles glowed from silver holders. She picked up her cocktail in the hand-blown martini glass Tang had bought as a Christmas present last year. "Did you finish your book?"

Heat rushed to Tang's cheeks. "Not yet. I've been given a one-week extension."

"What about Aaron? Is he covering your clients for another week too?"

Guilt settled in Tang's stomach. A sour taste lingered in her mouth. "I talked to him this afternoon. He agreed to take care of everything if I upped his commission to fifty percent in the event he sells anything while I'm gone."

Layla whistled soft and low. "That's a lot to pay for a licensed assistant."

"I lose nothing unless he makes a sale." Tang carried the serving dishes from the kitchen. The smell of beef and butter filled the room. "We didn't get to talk much this morning. How was your trip to see your brother? Did you get everything done that you wanted?"

Shrugging, Layla sat at the head of the table and allowed Tang to serve her. "Nolan and I had an estate sale and donated whatever was left to The Salvation Army." She leaned forward and closed her eyes, breathing in the aromas. "Then, we signed the final papers releasing the house. The cleaners are coming today. The buyers are signing tomorrow. We should have our portions of the sale deposited by midweek." She sighed and set down her glass and unrolled her silverware from the napkin. "Nolan and I agreed he could have the car. I told him I only wanted him to scan the family photos and save them with shared access on the cloud."

Tang nodded and took a seat next to her. She unfolded the napkin and bowed her head to silently pray—an old habit she had carried with her from childhood. "Sounds like you accomplished everything you'd set out to do."

"Yes … and this meat is so tender." Layla closed her eyes and chewed. "Tastes better every time."

Smiling, Tang cut into the flaky crust surrounding the juicy tenderloin and brought a piece to her mouth. The moist beef almost melted on her tongue. "I'm glad you like it."

"*Love* is a better word." Layla turned toward her. "You, of all people, should know about choosing the right word." Tiny furrows deepened between her seagrass eyes. She swirled the martini, then took a sip. She stared down at her plate and pinched the stem of the glass. "I'm disappointed you didn't come with me.

I could have used the support." She released the glass and lifted her gaze. "You were supposed to have finished the book." Fine lines formed around her puckered mouth. "Or was that just an excuse?"

Bowing her head, Tang studied the age spots on Layla's broad, weathered hands. "I'm sorry you're disappointed. I wrote everything, except the ending." She lifted her face. "My weekend didn't go as planned." *How much to tell? How much to leave out?* "I have writer's block."

"You went for a run. That usually helps."

Oh, why can't I tell her? The truth lodged in the pit of her stomach, and the green beans turned stringy and tasteless in her mouth.

"I'm worried about us. We feel like strangers."

"Between my mother dying and that never-ending book you're writing, we've been stressed." The sharpness of her voice didn't match the softness of her fingers on the back of Tang's hand. "But things will change. I put in my two weeks' notice. I'm retiring." She smiled and squeezed Tang's hand. "We'll have time to find each other again."

The tenderness crushed Tang. How dare she hope when all could be lost?

Chapter Ten

DEE
Fourteen Months Ago
San Francisco, California

One hour. One hour could change a life.

I'd brought Tang back to my hotel room with the paisley bedspread on the queen-size bed. The room had a desk by a window that overlooked Grace Cathedral and Nob Hill. In the background, the Golden Gate Bridge loomed like a picture on a postcard.

I lay, splayed out, naked, beneath the white sheet, my fingers playing in the tangles of Tang's hair. "You smelled like the ocean and tasted like oysters." I snuggled closer and nibbled on an earlobe. "I think I'm in love."

Tang rolled away. "How can you say those words when we don't know each other?"

I followed her like a shadow, clinging to her slick, warm body. "What do you want to know?"

Tang sat and glanced over her shoulder at me. "How old is your child?"

I stiffened. She must have noticed the pale silver lines zigzagging from my navel to my pubic hair. "I lost my son in childbirth."

"I'm sorry." Her voice sounded sad and far away.

"It was long ago." After the first lie, the rest became easy.

"Are you still with the father?" She frowned, waiting.

She wanted to know if I was single, available, and not interested in pursuing any other lovers, old or new, including men.

I could reassure her with another lie. "He left for someone who could give him a family."

"That must have been painful." Tang closed her eyes, then opened them. "Are you alone now? Or do you have someone waiting for you in New York?"

"Just my parents." I ran my hand against the smooth sheet. "I take care of them now that Chris moved away. They're selling our childhood home and moving into a new retirement community on Long Beach." I patted the space beside me, indicating I wanted her to come back to bed and stop this idle chitchat. "Have you ever been to Long Island?"

"I don't travel much."

A cell phone pinged from inside Tang's purse on the dresser beside the TV.

She strode over to the sound. Her naked body small and shapely, like a walking hourglass. After unzipping the purse, she pulled out the phone, typed a passcode then swiped a finger across the screen. "I must go. My ride's here."

I sat up and hugged the white sheet against my chest. "You should come to New York and visit me."

She stood before the mirror, zipping up a dress, shoving her feet into her shoes. She ran her fingers through her knotted hair. "I'd have to bring Layla." Rummaging around in her purse, she removed a bottle of perfume and sprayed it over her body. The cloud of wildflowers misted everywhere, filling the room with the false sense of spring.

"That's fine." I smiled. "I can tell her we're friends." The word sounded innocent and harmless. When she didn't respond, I added, "At least stay in touch. You have my number. Call or text anytime."

She slung her purse over one shoulder. "Good-bye, Dee."

"Wait. What about a kiss?" I stood and strode across the room, meeting her at the doorway.

I pressed my mouth against hers with the utmost gentleness and urgency. I needed her to remember the magic of our bodies, so she would be receptive to my plans of seeing her again.

Chapter Eleven

TANG
Fourteen Months Ago
San Francisco, California

"How was the conference?" Layla asked.

"Good." Tang tossed her suitcase into the backseat of Layla's hybrid sedan and slipped into the front passenger seat. Before tugging the seat belt across her lap, she leaned over and kissed Layla on the mouth, hoping the stick of gum she had chewed in the elevator and spat out in the lobby masked the briny taste of Dee.

"I'm glad you enjoyed it." Layla pulled away from the curb, navigating around the cars parked in the semicircular driveway. "I'm also glad you found an agent."

"Me too." Tang tensed her shoulders and stared at the hotel before it disappeared in the side-view mirror.

Layla hadn't complained about the way she tasted or the way she smelled. Either she hadn't noticed or she didn't care. Tang didn't know. She shifted her thoughts toward Dee, wondering if she would ever hear from her again.

"I have to rewrite the book to fit the new premise, but I have someone in my corner who will sell it once it's done."

"Rewrite?" Layla frowned, her fingers adjusting against the steering wheel. "I thought once you found an agent, the rest would be easy."

Tang chuckled. "Nothing about the publishing industry is easy." She clutched her hands in her lap and kept her gaze on Layla. "Maybe after the book sells, we can go to New York and meet the publisher and see the city."

"Maybe." Layla focused on the road, navigating the streets toward the Golden Gate Bridge. "Depends on work, my mother's health, and whether Aaron agrees to cover for you."

"Of course." Sighing, Tang pressed her back against the seat.

Layla always focused on practicalities.

Six years ago, Tang had needed a geotechnical engineer to assess a landslide on a property she had listed for sale. Another real estate agent in the office recommended the firm where Layla worked. Tang called and scheduled the appointment. A few days later, she met six-foot-tall Layla. She looked like a cowboy, dressed in a checked shirt and pressed jeans, but she shook hands like a wrestler. Tang had to take three steps in her black pumps to keep up with every one of Layla's in her work boots.

"Don't follow me," Layla had warned, waving her clipboard. "The ground isn't stable. I don't want you to hurt yourself."

Tang watched from the edge of the landslide, mesmerized by Layla's grace as she climbed down the slope and collected soil samples with a handheld drill. A week later, Layla presented her findings. The sellers agreed to the five-hundred-thousand-dollar repairs. By the time the property had sold, Tang and Layla had been a couple.

Now, their differences weren't as attractive. Biting her lower lip, Tang squelched the rising resentment that tasted bitter on her tongue.

"I'm sure Aaron will cover for me. But I understand your other concerns."

Stopped at a red light on Richardson Avenue, Layla let her hands fall from the steering wheel. "Why go to New York when you can meet online? Everyone does it nowadays."

"You're right."

The romanticism of the trip vanished. So did the potential complication of Layla meeting Dee and discovering there was more to their friendship. Despite the relief, Tang felt the loss as something palpable and real. Staring out the window at Crissy Field, she let her thoughts drift to the memory of Dee's mouth on the map of her body, the stops and starts, the twists and turns, the journey beginning and ending and beginning again. She shuddered with desire.

Would she ever see Dee again?

Chapter Twelve

TANG
Present Day
Bodega Bay, California

Clawing out of sleep, Tang blinked against the watery darkness in the bedroom. Layla breathed softly beside her. Quietly, Tang shoved her feet into her slippers, cinched the belt on her robe, and padded down the hallway into the kitchen.

She unplugged her phone from the charger and strained to read the screen. *No new messages*. The text she had sent to Dee yesterday was still marked as *Delivered*.

Where is Dee?

After brewing a pot of coffee, Tang took her steaming mug, sweetened with vanilla creamer, and settled into the chair beside her desk in the sunroom. With warm, trembling fingers, she booted up her laptop and searched for news of the woman who had died in the solo crash off Hangman's Bend.

Nothing.

She googled *Dee Young*.

Nothing.

She googled *Deidre James*.

Nothing.

She repeated the search in various combinations, including locations—from California to New York.

Nothing.

Sighing, she brought up the unfinished manuscript document and stared at the last paragraph she had written before Aaron called on Sunday.

The ghosts of the past haunted the present, but in a good way.

She stared at the blinking cursor, thinking of the story of an American man who believed in hard work and a Chinese immigrant woman who believed in luck, somehow finding their way to each other through the intercession of their dead parents. After a series of trials and tribulations, they came together again in the restaurant where they had gone on their first date. This scene was the final moment, the ending in which everyone was shown living happily ever after. But how could Tang write those final words when her own life had spun out of control?

Marcus reached his hand across the table and grasped Ya's fingers. "I wish my mother could have met you. She would have loved you."

But of course, she already knew her, and she already loved her. His mother was one of the spirits responsible for bringing them together. Marcus did not know this fact. Neither did Ya.

His mother's spirit hovered above the table. She leaned over Marcus's shoulder and whispered, "Ask her to marry you."

Tang stopped typing. She dropped her hands into her lap and thought. Layla had never asked Tang to marry her. And since Tang had met Dee, she had stopped nagging Layla about marriage. Why bother trying to persuade someone who didn't want to be persuaded? It was just like her book, only in reverse—Tang didn't have anyone in the afterlife rooting for her to get together with anyone. If she had, then maybe she would be sporting a diamond solitaire on her ring finger, or she would have flown to New York and met Dee's parents. No one in Dee's family, other than Christopher, knew she existed.

Christopher. That was who she needed to call.

In the browser, she googled *Christopher Young, San Francisco, writer*. Within seconds, she found his contact information.

"How's the writing?" Layla hovered in the doorway, one hand clasping a mug of coffee, the other hand waving the local paper.

Tang swiveled, minimizing the screen. Her heart lurched in her chest. "Fine. I just started."

"Thanks for making coffee." Layla took a sip and settled on the sofa, placing the paper on the coffee table. "I'm stopping by the store on the way home to pick up dinner for tonight. Do you need anything?"

"No, thanks." Tang clutched her hands in her lap and ground her molars. She glanced at her phone beside the scrap of paper where she had jotted Christopher's contact information. How could she find an excuse to leave and call Christopher? Who cared if it was only six o'clock? Dee was missing.

Layla unfolded the paper and leaned forward, scanning the headlines between sips of coffee. "The art festival is happening in two weeks. Are we going this year?"

After gulping down the rest of her lukewarm coffee, Tang stood and waved the empty mug. "I'll be right back. I need more coffee." She slipped her phone and the piece of paper into a pocket of her robe and shuffled out of the room. In the corner by the kitchen sink, she dialed Christopher's number. The call rolled over to voice mail.

"You've reached 4-1-5 ..."

Tapping her foot, she waited for the beep. "Christopher, it's Tang. Dee's friend. We met at a restaurant in San Francisco over a year ago. I was at a writers conference, and Dee was visiting. You and I had Hemingways." She lowered her voice. "Anyway, I'm calling because Dee and I had a fight over the weekend, and I haven't heard from her. I'm wondering if you've talked to her. I'm worried. Please call me at 7-0-7 ..."

She ended the call and tucked the phone into her pocket and poured another cup of coffee with vanilla creamer. When she returned to the sunroom, she halted, almost spilling her coffee.

Layla sat at Tang's computer, squinting at the screen. "Who's Christopher Young?"

Tang slurped the sloshing coffee that scalded her tongue. *Think, think, think.* "Someone I met at the writers' conference." The lie rolled effortlessly from her lips. "I remembered we were working on similar projects." She placed a hand on Layla's shoulder and squeezed. "Since I'm stuck, I was hoping he could help me brainstorm the ending."

"How come you've never mentioned him before?"

With a sharp intake of breath, Tang cupped the mug with both hands. "I'm desperate to finish. My deadline was only extended for one week. I never thought of reaching out to him until this morning." She nodded to the computer screen. "That's why I had to look him up. I didn't have his phone number."

Layla clicked out of the browser and read the last page of the unfinished story. Slowly, she swiveled in the chair, dropping her hands to her lap. "Why doesn't Marcus ask Ya to marry him?"

Tossing back her head, Tang laughed. "I can ask the same question of you." She stomped over to the cool windows overlooking the angry waves beyond the bay and clutched the warm mug against her chest. "If you can answer that question for me, then Marcus can answer that question for Ya." She half-turned, waiting, her eyes narrowed into slits.

Layla stood, her hands open and her arms outstretched. "I didn't know you still wanted to get married. You've acted so aloof these past few months that I assumed you didn't care anymore."

I had Dee to distract me. She's distracting me now.

"I still care." Tang finished turning around and took a step toward Layla. "I just stopped nagging."

With two more steps, Layla took the mug out of her hands and smiled. "I told you to come with me to Vermont." She set the mug on the coffee table and straightened. "The change of scenery would have done you good." Mouth warm against the ear, she whispered, "I got up early, hoping you'd still be in bed."

With the callous pads of her fingers, she brushed away the bangs from Tang's forehead and planted a kiss at a temple. Her other hand traced the swell of a breast.

Sighing, Tang felt a knot of tension unravel deep in her belly. Any thoughts of Dee or Christopher or her unfinished story melted away. She closed her eyes and leaned into Layla's warm caress.

***

Hours later, Tang watered the plants on the deck. The fog had burned off. The sky was blue and calm, the sun mild and warm against her back. A trill of music rang from the cell phone tucked into a back pocket. She turned off the water. Forgetting to check the caller ID, she swiped a finger across the screen. A nervous buzz jolted through her.

"Tang Young speaking."

"Hey, Tang. It's Aaron. I know you're supposed to be writing, but I really need your advice."

Aaron, her assistant.

"Of course." Only temporary relief. She sank into a lounge chair and stretched out her legs, her gaze focused on the waves. "Go ahead. Ask away."

"I'm having problems with the Parkers." He sighed. "Last week, they wrote an offer on a property, and they were outbid. How can I reassure them the outcome might be different this time?"

A common situation. Tang had seen similar things happen years ago, at the height of the market before the Great Recession. "Advise them to write their best offer first. Don't leave anything on the table."

"That's what they did last time." The frustration strained his voice thin.

"Okay, that's good." Thinking, she closed her eyes. "Obviously, it wasn't enough. So, this time, I want you to have them add a clause, stating they will pay five thousand more than the highest offer, not to exceed whatever amount they are willing to spend over and above the asking price."

"But if they write the offer for the maximum they can spend, how can they offer five thousand more than the highest bidder?"

"Easy. You press them. Ask if they can borrow money from other sources—an advance against wages, a 401(k), a kind and generous relative. Usually, people have some emergency funds they can draw from that they didn't even think of because they don't consider homebuying an emergency. But this is a seller's market, and they know it since they've already lost a potential dream home." She opened her eyes, knowing she should talk to the

Parkers and reassure them. "When are you meeting? I could come by and help you write the offer."

"But if you assist, then I'll lose my fifty percent commission, right?"

She ran a hand through her hair and squinted at the sunlight glittering on the water. "If you lose the sale, you get nothing."

"But I want to close this one on my own," Aaron pleaded. "I've worked so hard with them."

"I hear your frustration. I've felt the same way before."

"Then, you understand why I want to do this alone."

"I also know you have a lot working against you—the Parkers' doubt about your ability and your experience." She tightened her grip on the phone. "I suggest you observe how I handle this transaction. Then, you'll be better prepared next time."

"I appreciate the offer, Tang, but I need to close this deal on my own." He lowered his voice. "My wife isn't returning to work until after the baby is born. She's too scared after getting sick this weekend. I need the commission."

Tang stood. She had never been pregnant. But she imagined, if she had been pregnant, she might want to play it safe and stay home. Just like Aaron's wife wanted. She strode to the edge of the deck and grabbed the railing, clutching the phone against her ear.

"I understand. I'll let you handle this one on your own. Good luck." She smiled. "I'm here if you need me."

"Thanks, Tang."

She ended the call and tucked the phone into her back pocket. The salty air whipped her hair across her flaming cheeks.

Dee was a mother. No, Deidre was a mother. To Tyler. Tyler James.

She tightened her hold on the railing, feeling the rough wood pierce her skin with a splinter. Removing her hand, she plucked the sliver from her palm and tossed it over the deck. A drop of blood oozed to the surface of her skin. She licked the metallic taste with her tongue.

Christopher had never called her back.

Maybe I'll never know what happened to Dee. A dark cloud of emptiness shrouded her thoughts. *Maybe I'll never see her again.*

***

That evening, at seven, the doorbell rang.

"Welcome." Tang opened the blue front door and ushered Robin and Bert inside the warm foyer. She embraced the men, one after the other.

"I brought the red Layla liked last week," Robin said, holding up a bottle.

He was a tall, wiry man with grizzled white hair, cropped short around his ears, his hands as long and gnarled as tree roots.

"Thanks." Tang cradled the bottle and nodded toward the dining room. "Dinner will be served inside tonight. It's too cold to eat on the deck."

"Next week will be different." Robin frowned, shaking his head. "I heard on the news a weeklong heatwave starts tomorrow. The entire North Bay will have record highs in the low hundreds," he grumbled, rubbing his hands together. "The tourists will be clogging the roadways and the beach." Muttering obscenities, he strolled out of the foyer.

Tang turned to follow.

"You have a moment?" Bert asked.

Pausing in the doorway, Tang glanced over her shoulder. "Yes?" She held her breath, waiting.

Bert loomed in the narrow space with his hands thrust into his pockets. He rocked forward on his toes and sucked on his teeth. "Thought you should know they identified the body. They're contacting the next of kin before they release news to the public."

Tang gripped the bottle tight against her chest, like a baby about to fall. Her jaw tensed as she thought of Dee. "Parents? Or a brother?"

"I don't know."

42

The uncertainty plunged Tang into a new round of confusion. She loosened her grip against the bottle. Maybe she would never know.

Bert rubbed her shoulder. "She's probably a stranger."

"You're right." Tang led him to the dining room and set the bottle on the table. With a polite excuse, she left to retrieve the corkscrew in the kitchen.

"Hey, you're looking better." Layla grabbed the wineglasses from the cabinet. "Good day writing?"

Tang rifled through the drawer by the stove. "No, I'll get there. Eventually. I have a few days."

Layla set the wineglasses on the counter and hooked an arm around Tang's waist. "You still want to get married?"

An uncomfortable warmth flooded her body, and Tang wiggled out of the embrace. "It doesn't matter what I want."

"Of course it does." Layla bent and kissed her.

The taste of hope filled Tang's mouth.

Parting, Layla tilted her head and offered a smile. "You've made me open to the possibility."

"Really?" Tang searched her face, trying to see beyond the glitter of those sea-green eyes.

Nodding, Layla picked up the wineglasses and strode out of the room.

What changed? Tang bowed her head and rummaged around another drawer. Searching, she found the corkscrew buried beneath a small hill of measuring spoons and cups. Armed, she strode into the dining room, full of Robin's laughter and Bert's jokes. She opened the wine and filled the glasses and sat for the toast.

"To friendship," Bert said, lifting his glass.

"And good food." Robin winked.

"And love," Layla said.

"I'll toast to all that." Glancing from one face to another, Tang clicked her glass with the others. *And for people who are who they say they are.*

Chapter Thirteen

DEE
Thirteen Months Ago
Upper West Side, New York City, New York

After leaving San Francisco, I texted Tang every morning on the subway to work.

—Good morning, hot stuff.—

Tang always responded within moments.

—Good morning.—

Tang always ended her texts with a winky face emoji.

Once a week, I would video-chat with Tang. I always waited until Ryan and Tyler left for their bike ride around Central Park. As soon as I was alone, I would sit in the living room, my laptop on the coffee table, and indulge in my fantasy life for twenty minutes. I made up elaborate stories about the high-maintenance parents I had, who acted more like children than adults, and people I had to supervise and care for, who kept me bound to my life in New York even though I swore I'd always dreamed of living on the West Coast, in San Francisco, like my brother, who I envied for daring to escape, leaving me with all the responsibilities.

Most importantly, I would listen to Tang—to make her feel special, to make her understand how much I cared.

"I'm writing every day before work," Tang said. "I'm hoping to have the first draft to my agent in the next six months."

"That's great," I said. "I wish I had a creative project to work on. I've been so busy with pushing this new product and taking care of my parents."

"Where are you now?" Tang frowned.

"At home. But I'll be leaving soon to visit my parents." I groaned. "I don't want to go. I'll only be swamped with to-do lists. Dad is always starting a home improvement project he never

44

finishes, and Mom is always cooking food I can't eat." I scrunched my face. "I swear, you can't even feed her food to the homeless— it's so bad."

"Are you a better cook?"

"No, but I know how to order takeout." I grinned and touched my chest with my newly painted nails. "I accept my limitations."

"I'd love to meet your parents someday," Tang said.

I remembered Tang had mentioned losing her adoptive parents. She probably missed being part of a family, but I had no intention of introducing her to mine. Meeting Christopher was already too much information, but I would use that knowledge to my advantage.

"I have a work trip planned in October. I'll be staying with Chris, but I can drive up to see you. Will you be around?"

Tang checked the calendar on her desk. From what I could see on my laptop screen, she sat with her back to a window facing a parking lot. I assumed she was alone at work.

"I can schedule you in as a client. You could get a hotel. We could make love all afternoon."

A client. I twirled my hair, thinking. "I like the idea of you taking me to vacant properties. We can make love on the railing of a deck overlooking a private backyard. Or on the kitchen counter. Or in the bathroom." I softened my voice and my gaze. "So many possibilities."

A pink color stained her cheeks. She looked so cute when she was embarrassed. She fumbled with her hands. Her voice stuttered, "We—we won't have much time. The showings are timed for fifteen minutes. It's a tight market, especially during the weekends when everyone is home."

"I'll stop by during the week." A tightness stirred in my lower belly, and a pressure built between my legs. "We'll make it work, I promise."

A key jangled in the lock.

Oh shit, they're home early. Something must have happened.

"I need to go." I forced out the words in a rude rush. "Talk more this week." I blew a kiss and snapped the laptop closed just before Tyler ran into the room, flinging his arms around my neck and pressing his cold nose against my cheek.

Chapter Fourteen

TANG
Thirteen Months Ago
Bodega Bay, California

Every evening during dinner, Layla asked, "How's the book coming along?"

Tang pushed her wild rice to one side of the plate, feeling guilty and excited. "I wrote a great scene today between Marcus and Ya." She waved her fork above the tender calamari steak. "In the romance industry, the first encounter between the hero and the heroine is called the meet-cute." She set aside her fork. "Marcus is looking for an apartment. Ya's building has an opening. Marcus's mother, who's a ghost, suggests the building's owner place a flyer, advertising the vacancy, in the coffee shop where Marcus gets his daily coffee. Marcus sees the ad and makes an appointment for a viewing. When he's in the lobby, he runs into Ya, who's leaving for work, dressed in a suit and carrying a briefcase. He mistakes her for the property owner, and the fun begins."

Layla nodded, pouring another glass of wine. "I guess you could say our meet-cute was the landslide." She winked.

And my meet-cute with Dee was the restaurant in San Francisco. Tang brushed aside the thought and picked up her fork. "You're right. Our meet-cute wasn't conventional."

"And it wasn't influenced by any dead ancestor."

Neither was my meet-cute with Dee. Tang nodded, cutting into the calamari steak. The tender, buttery meat melted against her tongue.

"What happens next?" Layla leaned closer.

After swallowing, Tang shrugged. "I don't know. I'll find out tomorrow when I write the next chapter."

"You don't have an outline?"

Heat inched up Tang's neck. She couldn't tell Layla the truth. *I text Dee, and she offers a suggestion.* She never told Layla about the stranger she had met in the bar who inspired her to rewrite her story, the same stranger with whom she had embarked on an affair. How could she mention her now in this casual conversation? And yet how could she make something up?

"That's not how my process works."

"Winging it doesn't sound very effective or very professional."

"The professionals call it pantsing or discovery writing."

Layla shook her head and crumpled her napkin. "I don't understand creatives. In my industry, there are rules and regulations, standard operating procedures, common problems and solutions." She frowned, twisting the paper in her hands. "But you stare at a blank computer screen and just pants your way through a story. Incredible."

Incredible indeed. That wasn't how Tang went about writing, and Layla was right to suspect something more. But Tang vowed to never tell her or anyone about the woman who fed her lines, helping her build her story one word at a time.

Chapter Fifteen

TANG
Present Day
Bodega Bay, California

Tang sat at her desk, typing.

"Will you marry me?" Marcus asked, opening a tiny blue box.

Ya gaped at the diamond solitaire.

A faint voice whispered in her ear, "He's not the man he says he is. He's in debt from gambling, and he has a girlfriend on the side, who lives out of the country."

The cursor blinked like an enemy.

I want to kill him, *Ya thought. But she smiled and said,* "Yes."

"Ugh!" Tang slammed the laptop shut, pacing the length of the sunroom.

Outside, the light burnished like a fine line against the horizon. No fog. She grabbed her phone off the coffee table, swiped the screen, scrolled through her Contacts, and deleted the formerly blocked number and the text message that still said *Delivered.*

Done.

With a sigh, she returned the phone to the coffee table. After sinking into the sofa cushions, she leaned forward on her elbows and rubbed the heels of her palms against her misting eyes. *Why don't I feel better?* She would have to try and write an appropriate ending to the book alone. Not the one she had just written, full of anger and bitterness.

The floorboards creaked, and Layla entered the room, holding a mug of coffee. "Are you all right?" She sat beside her, placing a warm hand on Tang's cool knee.

"Yeah, just stuck, as always," Tang lied, lowering her hands into her lap.

"Why don't you go for a run before it gets too hot?" Layla rubbed her fingers back and forth across Tang's skin.

"Good idea." Getting out of the house would be an effective excuse to not write and a great distraction from thinking about Dee. "You're brilliant."

Smiling, Layla patted her arm. "I'm not brilliant. I just know you."

The depth of love reflected in those sea-green eyes haunted Tang. Would Layla be so generous and forthcoming if she knew the real reason why Tang wasn't writing? Or would Layla withdraw, like the absent fog on the horizon, dispersing her love like foam on the waves, the memory of their coupling like salt in the wind?

***

An hour later, breathless and sweaty, Tang strode through the kitchen for a glass of water before taking a shower.

Layla stood at the window, reading the paper. "They identified the person who died in the crash on Monday."

Nodding, Tang turned on the faucet and filled a glass with cool water. She took three long gulps, remembering what Bert had told her. *"She's probably a stranger."*

Layla folded the paper in half and pointed to the paragraph. "Thirty-nine-year-old Deidre James of New York. Her husband and son claimed her body yesterday."

Deidre James. Tang choked twice, gasping. Her hand shook when she set the glass on the counter.

Glancing over at the newsprint, she read the article.

The Sonoma County Sheriff identified the woman who died after the truck she had been driving plunged off a cliff on Highway 1 in Bodega Bay. Investigators stated the woman was under the influence of alcohol at the time of the crash.

50

Deidre James, 39, of New York, is survived by her husband, Ryan James, 41, her son, Tyler James, 8, her twin brother, and her parents.

"Isn't that horrible?" Layla asked.

Nodding, Tang glanced away. *She's dead.* The shock of the news numbed her fingers. No wonder Dee never responded. No wonder Christopher never called her back. He was probably too busy dealing with the authorities and Dee's family. Why would he care to talk with the woman with whom Dee was having an affair?

"They should put up a warning sign in both directions before that curve." Shaking her head, Layla flicked her wrist against the paper. "The guardrail and the speed limit are not enough."

Tang bobbed her head in agreement. But inside, her world had shifted, the tectonic plates sliding underneath everything she had ever known, burying the events of the past fourteen months under a landslide of facts.

Dee had been married.

She'd had a child.

And she didn't want me to know.

Chapter Sixteen

DEE
Ten Months Ago
Upper West Side, New York City, New York

"Mommy's traveling to California to see if she can buy us a house on a hill overlooking the ocean, sweetheart," I told the lie to Tyler as he was lying on my lap, watching TV. With my fingers, I brushed the hair from his forehead, the blond strands gleaming like threads of white gold.

I had been home for three weeks—a rare situation—and the monotony of domestic life was burning a hole through my skin. Not even my daily flirtations across the country with various love interests could sate my need for variety and control. I needed more. I needed Tang.

"I don't want to move," he said, his eyes focused on the screen. The sounds of the cartoon filled the room with commotion—fake car chases, skidding tires, squealing brakes, loud voices, and moments of odd silence.

"We aren't moving," I reassured him. "We'll have a second place to go on vacation."

"Will Nana and Pop-Pop join us?"

I sighed, thinking of Ryan's parents, who lived down the street in an apartment three blocks from Central Park. My own parents, long gone to Florida, never visited. And we only saw them once or twice a year when Chris convinced us to rent a condo with him for the holidays.

"No, this house will be just for you and me and Daddy. We'd take a plane and see Uncle Chris. Then, we'd drive north to our beach house."

"Will I see mermaids?" He had read a series of chapter books about magical sea creatures with his friend Melissa, and the idea of mermaids seemed like the only reason for him to join us on our adventure.

"Maybe." I didn't want to lie to him, but I didn't want to break his heart with the truth.

He blinked, and his eyelashes flickered with the colored lights from the TV. "Okay."

One word. Two syllables. The only confirmation I needed to justify everything that followed.

Chapter Seventeen

TANG
Ten Months Ago
Bodega Bay, California

Tang arrived early at the real estate office, pulling up listings, mostly vacant houses staged with furniture. She wanted to impress Dee, and she wanted the guarantee of privacy. Most of all, she wanted to create the perfect environment for anything to happen.

After the bell chimed in the lobby and the receptionist announced Dee's arrival, Tang ran a hand down the black dress suit she wore, grabbed the sheaf of papers from her cluttered desk, and strode into the stark conference room.

Dee sat on a chair, dressed in a white blouse and black skirt. She crossed her long, slender legs, her signature red lipstick a dash across her lips. As soon as she noticed Tang, she stood, glancing all around before embracing her. "My baby," she whispered.

Tang clutched her like a pillow after a nightmare, the length of their bodies fitting perfectly together. "Oh, Dee-Dee." She sighed. "It's so good to feel you again."

"Likewise." Dee released her slowly. The air rushed in to fill the space, a buzz of molecules jumping from excitement. "I like your workplace. It's so close to the ocean I can even smell the salt in here."

Nodding, Tang scanned the length of Dee's body—from her red heels to long blonde hair. "You haven't changed."

"Thanks." Dee smiled and winked. "You're more beautiful."

A sizzle of heat zipped up Tang's back and spread across her shoulders and down her arms to warm her hands. She gestured to the doorway. "Ready to go look at some houses?"

"I've been looking forward to it all week." Dee strode past, pinching Tang's butt as she exited the conference room.

I hope no one saw. Tang scanned the hallways, only seeing the rush of real estate agents ducking into the copy room or sliding into office chairs behind desks in a bank of cubicles, their headsets tight against their ears, their voices a low chatter like the rush of waves at high tide.

Outside, the wind blew her hair across her face. Tang wiped her fingers across her eyes and squinted. "We'll take my car," she said, pointing to a red compact vehicle toward the back of the lot.

"Not a luxury vehicle?" Dee asked. "I thought you were a top producer."

"I am, but I'm also frugal." Tang pressed the fob and unlocked the doors. "Why own a vehicle that will only rust from the saltwater air?"

The four-door sedan had recently been detailed at a car wash in Santa Rosa. The inside smelled like a pine forest, the leather polished, smooth and slippery, and the outside gleamed like a shell.

"Five houses, fifteen minutes each," Tang said, tugging the seat belt across her waist.

Dee grimaced. "I thought California was more laid-back than New York."

Glancing over her shoulder, Tang backed up in the gravel lot and shifted into drive. "In this high-demand market, our real estate association decided to time the lockboxes for efficiency."

"What can you do in fifteen minutes?" Dee leaned against the door with her gaze focused on the bay.

Tang braced her shoulders, slowing for a curve along the highway. "You get a general impression of the property. If you like it, you write an offer. If the offer is accepted, you have a certain time period for inspections. You can stay as long as you'd like then, taking in all the details."

"You know I don't plan on buying anything," Dee said.

"Then, why didn't you just rent a hotel room overlooking the ocean?" Tang signaled, turned left, and drove up the road

55

toward a newer subdivision. "We could have made love in comfort all afternoon."

"Then, how would you explain my visit to Layla?" Dee turned to face her. "And how would I have explained my need for Chris's truck?"

"You could have lied." Tang pulled into the driveway of a beach house with floor-to-ceiling windows, opening to a deck. She unclicked her seat belt, her eyes narrowing into slits. "No one would have known the difference."

Dee heaved her shoulders in a sigh. "I'm not that type of woman."

"Then, what type of woman are you?" Tang shifted, and her hips slipped against the polished leather. "I had to go through hours of preparation, previewing homes and making sure they were vacant and staged." She paused, a rush of frustration pulsing in her temples. "I had to coordinate showing times to coincide with driving times." She clenched her fists, and a muscle in her jaw flexed. "I could have split the difference for the cost of a hotel room. You could have parked in the real estate lot, and we could have taken my car to your room."

Dee opened the door. A swoosh of salty air blew between them. "We've already lost five minutes."

Gaping, Tang watched Dee saunter up the paved path to the front door, her long blonde ponytail sweeping across her narrow back.

I don't understand her. She isn't being reasonable.

Tang clambered out of her seat and into the rush of wind, jangling her keys, her purse sliding from her shoulder. At the front door, she jostled past Dee, fitted her lockbox key into the receptacle, and punched in her number. Three beeps later, the shackle released, and a dull metal key fell into her palm. She unlocked the front door and stepped aside, waving Dee into the house that smelled as damp and musty as a high school gym locker.

In the family room, a wall of windows faced a grove of cypress trees.

Dee spun from the sight and padded across the carpet, reaching for Tang's hands. "I'm sorry I upset you." She pulled her forward until they stood nose to nose in the center of the room, staged to look like a family might gather around the TV to watch a late-night movie after dinner. "Please, forgive me."

Dee ran the tips of her fingers up Tang's spine until they brushed against the nape of her neck and tangled in the strands of dark hair against her scalp. Dipping her head, Dee angled her lips to fit against Tang's mouth.

Anger melted into desire and pooled in the bottom of Tang's stomach. She reached up, encircling her arms around Dee's body, tugging her close, until their breasts pressed against each other. The never-ending kiss released a flood of warmth to the surface of her skin.

Bleep, bleep.

The timer on Tang's phone rang.

Stepping back, Dee released her hold. "Next house?"

Gasping and nodding, Tang led the way back outside and locked the front door. The wind had died down, leaving an eerie hush, the air stagnant and briny.

At the next house—a Frank Lloyd Wright design sculpted into the side of a cliff—Tang followed Dee into the kitchen.

Dee ran her fingers across a boulder carved into an island. "Is this real?"

"Genuine," Tang said. "Just like the waterfall in the living room."

"Amazing." Dee pressed Tang's back against the rough boulder and kissed her shoulder, slipping her hands underneath her blouse and cupping her breasts against the lace bra.

Tang squirmed, careful not to gouge her skin against the sharp protrusions.

The buzzer rang before Dee could unhook Tang's bra.

At the third house, Tang led Dee into the master bedroom and sucked her breasts beneath a skylight.

Dee arched her back and groaned, her long, painted nails digging into Tang's shoulders.

The buzzer rang as Tang's hands traveled below Dee's waist, grazing the seam of her underwear.

At the fourth house, Dee tugged Tang into the hall bathroom and closed the door. She pressed Tang's back against the wall and reached underneath her dress, tugging the underwear down her legs until they circled her ankles.

Tang stepped out of the underwear, feeling a draft between her legs.

Dee folded the underwear and tucked it into her purse. She knelt on the blue rug and shimmied the skirt over Tang's hips, exposing her mound. Smiling, she glanced up at Tang's face before lapping between her legs, a slow trickle of moisture beading at her lips.

The buzzer rang.

"Don't stop." Tang curled her fingers into Dee's hair and tugged her closer, closer.

Dee pulled away before Tang came. She tugged the skirt over Tang's hips and stood, kissing her.

"Why did you stop?" Tang gasped between the salty taste mingling with their tongues.

Releasing her, Dee stepped back and opened the bathroom door. "I like teasing you." She smiled, flashing her teeth, her red lipstick smeared on her glistening cheeks and chin.

"More like torture," Tang grumbled, wobbling on unsteady knees through the maze of the house. The fire in the pit of her lower stomach burned, and the ache between her legs pulsed with a dull throb.

Oh, how much longer till the next and final house?

In the car, Dee pulled down the visor and checked her face in the tiny mirror. From her purse, she withdrew a package of baby wipes and rubbed off the makeup around her mouth. "These are amazing," she said as she worked. "I ran out of makeup wipes when I was visiting my brother when my nephew was a baby, and I was desperate, so I tried one of these. They worked so much better. I've used them ever since."

Tang drove down the hill, pulsing the brakes. "Tell me about your nephew. I didn't know Chris had a son."

"Tyler just turned eight." Dee snapped the visor shut and zipped up her purse. "He's a cutie."

"Do you have any pictures?" Tang had never wanted children, but Layla had, years ago, before they met.

Layla had even married a man, hoping to get pregnant, but the marriage had crumbled, and the pregnancy never happened.

"I'm sure I do." Dee rummaged in her purse, pulled out her phone, and scrolled.

Tang turned down a street. A row of houses perched above the highway, the rush of the traffic sounding like surf through a chink in the window.

"I guess I don't."

With a sidelong glance, Tang frowned.

Dee shoved the phone back into her purse. "His mom has him eighty percent of the time anyway, and I hardly see him anymore, except for holidays." Sighing, she hugged her purse toward her chest. "Any kids in your life?"

"No." Tang drove into a gravel driveway and cut the engine. "I was adopted. No siblings. Unless my birth parents had additional children." The taste of bitterness clung to her tongue.

She hated talking about the family she didn't have anymore. Most people she knew had relatives they knew about even if they didn't get along or see each other much. But she was alone. She had been alone since her parents had died in an automobile accident when she was in her twenties, just after graduating from college with a degree in business administration. After burying her parents, she earned her real estate license, sold the house she had grown up in, and rented an apartment, holding on to the funds for an uncertain future. By the time she had met Layla, she had given up on anything beyond the moment.

Even now, in the heat of the car, with the ticking engine cooling in the driveway of somebody else's home, and with Dee beside her, warm and present and still, she sensed the hollowness of her existence like the inside of a bell.

Bowing her head, she rested her brow against the leather steering wheel and closed her eyes. "I don't know if I can endure this anymore."

"Don't worry." Dee rubbed her upper back with a soft and gentle hand. "I'll satisfy you." She clicked open the door, and a swell of sea salt wafted inside.

Slowly, Tang opened her eyes and lifted her head. Why was she here with this woman she hardly knew, having sexual adventures in what her colleagues would refer to as inventory? She shook her head. "I can't."

"I told you I would make you come." Dee slipped her purse over her shoulder and flashed a coquettish smile. "Let's go." She flicked her wrist toward the house—a brown-shingled cabin hidden behind scrub bushes and medicinal-smelling eucalyptus trees.

For a long moment, Tang considered her options. Leave Dee here, swearing to never see her again, and return to the real estate office and send her assistant, Aaron, to come pick her up. But how would she explain leaving an out-of-town client alone at a vacant house in a foreign city? She couldn't.

Dee stood in the walkway, arms crossed over her chest, her red mouth a pout. *I'm waiting*, she mouthed.

Maybe Tang could leave the car and enter the cabin, circling around the floor plan, avoiding Dee's flirtation. But the memory of Dee's hands on her body set her skin on fire. How could she stop feeling helpless around her?

Finally, Dee stalked over to the driver's door and yanked it open. With her cool, slim hands, she tugged on Tang's arm, leading her out of the car. With her hip, Dee shut the door.

The aggressive move jolted Tang into compliance. She followed Dee up the narrow path to the front door. She released the key from the lockbox and set the timer on her phone. Once inside the dark, moist cabin, Tang turned on the lights and strode into the kitchen with its single window overlooking the bay. The water was still and glassy, a blue mirror reflecting the peaceful sky.

Dee sidled up behind her, rolling Tang's skirt up over her buttocks and parting her legs. "Resistance is futile." She slid her fingers inside the warm, damp cavern.

Gasping, Tang clung to the counter. Her legs quivered, and her breath quickened. No slow tease, building up and halting. Just fingers and tongue moving fast and faster. No stopping now. She

60

closed her eyes, threw back her head, and screamed. A wet trickle dribbled down the inside of her leg, and she collapsed forward, her hands still gripping the counter, her heartbeat thumping, even as her breath eased back into a normal rhythm.

The timer in her purse rang, and she pawed at her skirt.

"Just a moment." Dee stood and removed a package of baby wipes and Tang's underwear from her purse.

Tang dabbed the wet cloth between her legs and rubbed another one down the inside of her thighs before slipping into her underwear. She wobbled on sea legs through the cabin, flipping off lights, securing the door, and returning to the car, where she sat, stunned by the power of the orgasm. A radiant warmth suffused her skin.

Before turning the key in the ignition, she glanced at Dee. "What about you?"

Shrugging, Dee let a slow smile curl her red lips. She leaned over and whispered, "Next time."

Next time.

A threat.

A promise.

Chapter Eighteen

TANG
Present Day
Bodega Bay, California

Humming, Tang sliced the mushrooms for the chicken marsala. Cooking occupied her the same way writing did—by taking up all mental space, so she could not focus on anything else, not even conversation. Luckily, Layla was taking a shower, having spent the day at some excavation or something or other after which she brought three feet of dirt home on her body, clothes, and boots.

After melting two tablespoons of butter, Tang placed the chicken breasts, coated with egg and flour and sprinkled with salt and pepper, into the sizzling pan and lowered the heat to let the chicken brown for five minutes. Turning back to the counter, she diced one shallot and minced two cloves of garlic.

"Mmm. Smells good." Layla wafted into the room, dressed in a clean button-down shirt and jeans, her bare feet on the hardwood floor. She leaned down to kiss Tang on the top of her head and reached behind her in the cupboard for a glass to fill with water from the sink. "My department is throwing a retirement party at the Villa restaurant in Santa Rosa next Friday night. I told them you'd be joining me." She gulped a mouthful of water and hugged the glass to her chest.

Tang smiled and scraped the chopped shallots and minced garlic into the bowl of sliced mushrooms. "Oh good. Then, I get a night off from cooking." She winked. Inside, she winced. She didn't like sitting at a table, surrounded by nature, science, and math geeks, but she didn't want to disappoint Layla. Especially not after the guilt she still felt over her affair with Dee. "Have you thought about what you plan to do during your retirement?"

Lifting her eyebrows, Layla tilted her head to one side. "Home improvements. The exterior of the house needs to be sanded and water-sealed, including the deck. Maybe change the outdated fixtures in the bathroom. And fix that sticky seal in the bedroom window." She leaned against the counter and shifted the weight between her feet. "The rest depends on you."

"On me?" Tang flipped the chicken breasts. What did she have to do with Layla's retirement? She still planned to work for another fifteen years.

"I want to go to Europe with you." Layla set her glass on the counter and took a step forward. "After you finish the book, of course."

"Why does the book need to be finished?" Tang set the timer on the kitchen oven, so she wouldn't lose track of time. Talking always distracted her. "I have a real estate business too."

"Winter is always slow for real estate. If we leave at the beginning of November, we can be back at the end of January."

"Three months?"

Layla nodded, her sea-green eyes glittering. "We'd rent houses in three different countries—England, France, and Italy."

Three months and three countries.

Tang sucked in a breath. "Who's paying?"

Neither one of them had saved enough for a luxury vacation.

"My inheritance. Once the estate is settled, I'll walk away with close to a million dollars." Layla lowered her voice. "I want to spend a little on us before investing the rest of it." She smiled. "Who knows? If your book is a bestseller, then maybe you can join me in retirement."

Tang laughed. "If my book does that well, my agent will want another book."

"You can write in France, like Hemingway."

The buzzer beeped.

Tang turned off the timer and removed the chicken on a paper towel–covered plate. In the leftover grease, she dumped the mushrooms, shallots, and garlic. She checked on the wild rice in the rice cooker and removed two prepared salads from the refrigerator. "That would be a dream come true. But I can't count on it."

"Why not?" Layla grabbed the bowls. "I can help you write the ending."

A pain squeezed in Tang's chest. "I appreciate the offer. But you're not even a reader."

"I will be as soon as I read your book." Layla padded out of the kitchen with the salads.

Tang stirred the mushrooms, shallots, and garlic until the mixture softened and browned. Then, she added the chicken and the marsala wine and chicken broth and covered the skillet to let the juices simmer.

On the counter, Tang's cell phone rang. As she wiped her hands on a towel, she glanced at the screen. A 415 area code jumped out at her. Her pulse lurched.

Layla strode back into the room. "Who's calling?"

"Christopher." Tang didn't want to lie anymore. After swiping the screen, she pressed the phone against her ear. "Can you hold just a second?" She swallowed, waiting for Layla to gather the plates and the silverware.

"You really think a guy you met once can help with your book?" Layla held the dishes close to her chest and wrinkled her forehead. "Why not someone who knows you?"

"He's a writer. You're not."

After a flash of a frown, Layla turned and left the room.

As soon as she was alone again, Tang lifted the phone. "Thanks for waiting." Her heartbeat knocked against her ribs, and her palms sweat.

"No problem. It's Christopher Young," he said. "In case your caller ID doesn't work. I'm sorry it took me so long to return your call."

"I understand." Tang glanced at the doorway, fearing Layla's imminent return. "I read the news. I'm sorry Dee's gone."

"Me too." He coughed. "It's been crazy busy with her family coming out."

"I can imagine." Tang clenched her jaw and tightened her grip on the phone. "Your sister didn't tell me she was married or had a son. She said Tyler was her nephew and that you were his father. I never doubted her. Why did she lie?"

Layla reappeared in the doorway.

"Hold on." Tang lowered the phone and lifted a finger. "Give me two minutes. Then, I'll bring out the food."

Nodding, Layla grabbed her glass of water and a stack of trivets and exited the kitchen.

Alone, Tang turned off the stove and the rice cooker. She hovered in the corner by the window, where the reception was best, and adjusted the phone against her ear. "Thanks again for waiting. I can't talk long. But I keep wondering what else I don't know about her."

"Can you meet?"

"Meet?" Tang had hoped they could exchange information over the phone or by email. Why did they have to meet? She listened to her tight breaths and wondered what she would tell Layla. How could she be honest without revealing all her past lies?

"Yes, in San Francisco," Christopher said. "I'll be flying out tomorrow night for the funeral in New York, but I can meet you for lunch at Pier 39. I'll be on the dock by the sea lions at twelve thirty. Okay?"

Tomorrow. She wasn't supposed to do anything but write. But she couldn't break through her block until she knew the truth about Dee. If Christopher would tell her. If he knew. If, if, if.

"Okay. I'll be there."

Chapter Nineteen

TANG
Nine Months Ago
Johnson, Vermont

Tang woke up in the guest bedroom and pulled back the lace curtains. Snow. A white blanket dusted the dirt around the forest of maple trees surrounding Jade Goodfellow's residence in this tiny town of locals who had gotten stuck here and never left. Since arriving the day before Thanksgiving, Tang marveled at the natural beauty, wondering how Layla could have wandered so far away, leaving this maple-syrup farm and her family.

"Good morning." Layla padded over to Tang and kissed her shoulder before pulling Tang against her chest and holding her tight. "Beautiful, isn't it?"

"I can't imagine why you left," Tang said, sinking into the warmth of Layla's body.

"You've never tapped a maple tree for sugar, have you?" Layla stiffened. "It takes forty gallons of sap to make one gallon of maple syrup, and each tree produces only ten gallons a year, if you're lucky. The boiling room is always hot. The whole process is so slow and tedious; it feels never-ending." She sighed. "When I was a kid, I'd wish for snow. Snow marked the end of the maple-syrup season. You can't tap a tree in the snow. You must wait till it's warm, so the sap flows."

Tang couldn't imagine working this farm year in and year out. Acres and acres of maple trees. Hours and hours of hard manual labor. Even though Layla drilled into the earth for soil samples, she didn't repeat the process daily for one season after another. She had other things to do, like administrative tasks, that left her body free from the repetitive strain her brother, Nolan, suffered, working on this family farm. Even Layla's mother—

eighty-five-year-old Jade—still boiled and bottled each season, overseeing production and assisting the clerks in the retail store.

"C'mon. Let's help cook the turkey." Layla released Tang and patted her bottom. "Last one downstairs has to baste the bird."

***

Tang wandered into the country kitchen. The scent of coffee and maple-syrup scones filled the warm air. Tang poured a cup of coffee and sweetened it with cream and sugar before approaching Jade—a small, hunched woman with a cloud of white hair—standing beside the counter, massaging butter against the turkey's back.

Tang asked, "Do you need any help?"

"Ah, honey, you just relax. Layla will be back in a moment to put the bird in the oven." Jade smiled, and her hazel eyes sparkled. "After you finish your coffee, you can peel potatoes. Layla will make the brussels sprouts. I already baked the pecan pie, and Nolan made pumpkin maple thumbprint cookies, just the way he's always made them since he was a kid but the thumbprints are bigger now." She winked.

Tang took a seat at the old wooden table and folded her arms on the doily tablecloth. She marveled at the sense of home she felt in this wallpapered kitchen with its oak cabinets and copper pots and handmade dish towels. Everything felt safe and secure. If she had grown up in this comfort, she would have never left. No matter how much work it was to tap a tree or boil sap or stand eight hours in a retail shop and listen to customers complain, she would have endured the hardship if she could come back and rest her feet on a wooden bench before the stove and sip a brandy, like she had watched Nolan do the night before—his eyes almost closed, the flicker of candlelight dancing on his unshaven cheeks, the strong scent of perspiration and hard work seeping from his pores and clinging to his woolen shirt and worn jeans, his stockinged feet crossed at the ankles. But she was a suburban girl, who had grown up in a boring subdivision in sunny California, where families broke apart and fell together like building blocks.

From her back pocket, Tang's cell phone rang. She glanced at the screen.

Dee.

"Who's calling, sweetie?" Jade asked.

Tang frowned, swiping the red button across the screen to send the call to voice mail. "Wrong number."

Nodding, Jade glanced out the window at the falling snow. "I don't approve of my daughter's lifestyle. I don't understand it, you know?" She washed her hands in the sink and dried them with a hand towel. "But I want to be a better mother because my children deserve to be happy, you understand?"

Tang bobbed her head in agreement and tucked the phone back into her pocket just as it pinged with a voice mail message.

"I want my children to be with good people." After tossing the towel on the counter, Jade turned and pinned Tang with a glower. Her hunched shoulders shook. "Are you an honest person?"

"Yes." The word left Tang's mouth like a reflexive gesture, the sting of the lie as hot as the coffee on her tongue.

***

While Layla and her mother washed the dishes from dinner, Tang followed Nolan into the family room.

He knelt beside the fireplace. "Do you know how to build a fire?"

Shaking her head, Tang knelt beside him.

"First rule: dry wood only." Nolan grabbed a split log from the stack beside the hearth.

Tang ran her fingers along the rough edges, careful to avoid getting a splinter.

"Second rule: lots of kindling." Nolan tossed a handful of pine cones, twigs, and smaller wood scraps on the stacked logs. "Third rule: just a hint of fire starter."

He wedged a roll of newspaper between the logs and kindling and, with a match, lit its jagged edge on fire. The bright flame sparked and flickered. Soon, a shimmering wave of red-and-gold tongues spit and hissed and crackled as they lapped up the sides of the wood.

Sitting back on his heels, he stared at his handiwork and nodded. "I love this season. Everything slows down."

Standing, Tang took a step back. She studied Nolan's profile—the broad forehead, the sharp nose, the bearded chin. He was large and quiet, almost contemplative. She imagined him working in the maple grove behind the house, tapping the trunks of trees, his boots clumping in the uneven soil, humming to himself and smiling. Just enjoying life.

Tang took another step back and wrapped her arms around her waist, frowning. "Why didn't Layla stay and work the family business?"

Nolan rose, casting a towering shadow across the hardwood floor. His knees creaked, and when he walked, his shoulders sloped, like his mother's. "She outgrew Johnson. Went to Boston for college. Got used to living by the bay." He blinked and swallowed. "Graduated. Joined a firm. Got a call to work in California. Lots of reclaimed land along the coast." Smiling, he faced Tang. "Layla always could patch things together. Didn't matter what it was. Soil, mud, rocks, rubble, and dirt. She found a way to shore up the land, make things right again." He scratched the skin beneath his grizzled beard. "She's something special. I hate living so far apart from her."

"Why did you stay?" Tang asked.

He wrinkled his brow and gave her a sidelong glance. "Somebody had to take care of Mama and the maple trees."

"Obligation," Tang said, glancing at the fire.

"Doing the right thing." Nolan took a seat in the recliner and crossed his ankles. "There's a difference. One is expected. The other isn't." He withdrew a pipe from his shirt pocket and unwrapped a package of tobacco. "Nobody asked me to stay. Nobody asked me to go. I'm here because I'm needed. And once I'm not needed anymore, I'll find another way to spend my days."

Tang nodded. "Did you ever want a family?"

After lighting a match and puffing until a small cloud lifted from the pipe, Nolan sank back against the cushions and exhaled.

The smoke smelled fragrant, almost sweet. From the kitchen, the clatter of pots and pans mingled with the rush of running water and the low murmur of conversation as Layla and Jade cleaned up.

Nolan glanced up at the wood-beamed ceiling. "I have a family."

Tang perched on the edge of the sofa and leaned forward, resting her arms against her knees. The warmth from the fire moved up her legs and into her lap. "I mean, a wife and kids."

He shook his head. "Why screw up something that's already perfect?"

"I don't know." Tang felt her cell phone vibrate in her back pocket. She clenched her jaw. Probably a text message from Dee since Tang never returned the voice mail from this morning. Tang shifted her hips, removed the phone, and swiped the screen.

—*Happy Thanksgiving.*—

Yes, Tang was right. The message was from Dee.

A stream of suggestive emojis followed the innocuous words.

"Family?" Nolan asked, eyeing the phone.

Shaking her head, Tang responded.

—*Happy Thanksgiving to you too!*—

Tang added a kissing face emoji.

"Friend," Tang said. "I don't have a family." She tucked the phone back into her pocket, her whole body flushed with hidden joy.

Chapter Twenty

TANG
Present Day
San Francisco, California

At first, Tang didn't recognize Christopher. His hair was darker than she had remembered—a caramel brown. He leaned on a railing overlooking the plank of sea lions barking and complaining, their slick bodies sliding over each other and spilling into the murky water. Squinting, she willed him to look at her. When he finally turned, she recognized the kind camaraderie in his dark brown eyes. He stood abruptly and strode toward her around a clot of tourists.

"Hey, thanks for coming." Smiling, he outstretched his hand. He was taller than Dee with broad shoulders and a narrow waist. The rank wind ruffled the collar of his tan sports jacket and rippled along his black slacks and scuffed leather shoes.

As she shook his hand, she stared at his long, tapered fingers—Dee's hands. "Long time no see." Tilting back her head, she offered him a crooked smile.

"I never expected to see you again after that night in the restaurant." He gestured to the sidewalk, moving away from the dock.

"I was actually hoping I'd see you sooner." Tang shoved her hands into her jacket and navigated past gift shops and food stands until the throngs of people thinned and the constant chatter lowered to a low buzz and the heavy scent of fried food gave way to smog and dirt and gasoline-powered traffic. "But Dee wouldn't let me come down to visit. She always insisted on coming up to see me." A dull pain squeezed her chest. "I can't believe I'll never see her again." She slowed her pace for a moment to catch her breath.

Christopher stopped two steps ahead and glanced over his shoulder. "Are you all right?"

She shook her head, her mouth numb.

He circled back and placed a hand on her shoulder. "Let's sit." He pointed toward an empty bench along the Embarcadero by the ferry building.

Nodding with gratitude, she sank against the steel frame and gazed out at the choppy water toward the gray Oakland Bay Bridge. The wind had finally quieted, and the gulls and pigeons that landed at her feet pecked at the crumbs left by a previous occupant.

She knotted her hands in her lap, shifting her gaze to meet his profile. "Did she tell you about her trip north?"

"She said she was looking at a vacation home for her family."

The real estate lie again. Shame doused her. "Weren't you worried when she hadn't returned the next morning?"

"No, I wasn't. I assumed she had gone directly to work." He hunched his shoulders. "But when I didn't see my truck in the carport that night, I knew something was wrong." He leaned back. "I don't know what impression my sister gave you, but I know her—*knew her*—as somewhat erratic." He swallowed and brushed the hair out of his eyes. "She was always troubled."

Troubled? "What do you mean?"

He stared at the water. "Her brain was wired differently. She saw everything as a game." He bowed his head and sighed. "I'm sorry you didn't know."

Tang stiffened. "You mean, she played me?"

A dark laugh escaped his throat. "She played everyone." He turned his gaze toward her. "But she could be good. She voted and volunteered. She was a great mother. Tyler never noticed the difference." He slouched forward and gazed at the bobbing waves. "I don't know what type of wife she was to Ryan, but he never complained. I suspect he knew she had problems. He must have accepted them."

A fierce sense of betrayal blazed underneath Tang's skin. "I didn't know she was troubled and had problems." Pressure built up behind her eyes. "Why didn't she tell me?"

He gave her a sidelong glance. "I don't know."

72

Frowning, Tang leaned forward and clasped her hands between her knees. She stared at the ferry floating toward the dock. "She said she had a stillborn child." She pursed her lips. "Why would she fabricate her past?"

"She liked her privacy."

"So do I, but I didn't lie to her." Tang sat up and released her hands. "Why couldn't she tell me the truth?"

She frowned, remembering their last meeting. *"Will you marry me?"*

A spike of hostility and anger pierced her chest. *She was already married.*

"I wish I had known." He raised his eyebrows and sighed. "I've gotten a handful of calls from other men and women, asking about her." He shifted on the bench to face her. "Seems like she had plenty of entanglements across the country. Mostly in the cities where she traveled for work. You weren't the only one."

Tang gasped. *I wasn't the only one.* The truth absorbed into the dry soil of her heart.

He clasped his hands. "I do know one thing: she had no intention of leaving her family."

The last fourteen months unraveled, one lie after another. *Dee was troubled. She had no intention of leaving her family.*

Tang frowned at the seagulls pecking at the sourdough breadcrumbs scattered by her feet. The pressure built behind her eyes. "I can't believe she asked me to leave my girlfriend and move to New York to marry her."

The wind bit into her cheeks. She struggled to breathe, to calm the internal storm.

"I'm sorry." He screwed up his lips and shook his head, his hair flapping across his forehead.

The repeated phrase did nothing to assuage the pain and rage flooding through her. She curled her hands into fists and rubbed her swollen eyes.

"Do me a favor," he said. "Don't contact Dee's husband or son. They don't need any more grief than they already have."

"And I do?" She dropped her hands into her lap and glowered.

"That's not what I mean." He leaned forward, jabbing his fists into his pockets, the wind rippling the fabric of his jacket. "You need to believe me when I say, she didn't mean to hurt you." The tone of his voice hushed into the murmur of waves. "She never meant to hurt anyone."

"How do you know?" She jutted her jaw and ground her molars. Pain flared in her chest.

He turned to face her. "Because we're twins."

Every muscle in her body stiffened. "Are you saying you're just like her—a player?" She held her breath, waiting for his reaction.

He shook his head, his expression softening. "No, I'm the *exact* opposite." His voice broke, and his dark brown eyes filled with tears.

More pain squeezed Tang's chest. Dee's lies had hurt everyone, including her brother. Her twin. The one person who had known her better than everyone else. Silently, Tang touched Christopher's arm, hoping to stop his tears.

***

Bodega Bay, California

"Did Christopher agree to help you finish your novel?" Layla asked that night at dinner.

Tang twirled her fork in a plateful of overcooked spaghetti. She had been too distracted, letting the water boil too long. The sauce, usually thick and spicy, was watery and tasteless. "Not really."

"Not really?" Layla echoed. "You spent the day in San Francisco. He could have told you over the phone he couldn't help."

"It's not that easy." Tang dropped the fork. It clinked against the table. Tomato sauce dribbled on the tablecloth. Muttering curses beneath her breath, she dabbed the red spots with her napkin. The stains smeared deeper into the fabric. "He agreed to help. It's just that he didn't have the answers I needed."

"Stop scrubbing. I'll bleach it." Layla swatted away Tang's hand. "I don't understand what's taking you so long. Can't your agent fix the ending?" Her voice rose to a dangerous pitch. A vein throbbed in her forehead. She picked up her glass, swirling the Pinot Noir. "I've been patient with this book of yours for too long." After taking a slug, she closed her eyes and steadied her voice. "Can't you just stick in the marriage proposal, have the other character say yes, and type *The End*?" She snapped her eyes open. "Do I need to write it for you?"

Tang stared into Layla's eyes. The pupils narrowed to tiny pinpricks. The irises exploded into a shock of green, flecked with yellow. Angry eyes, frustrated eyes, eyes that had waited too long for too little.

Tang quivered with fear. *I can tell Layla the truth, or I can make her happy.*

Almost instinctively, Tang dropped the napkin in her lap and reached for Layla's hand, the cool skin speckled with age spots. With a light squeeze, Tang smiled. "I'll finish the book tomorrow."

Chapter Twenty-One

TANG
Eight Months Ago
Bodega Bay, California

"Merry Christmas!"

Tang stepped into the kitchen, the scent of strong coffee brewing, and blinked at Jade, perched on a stool at the stovetop counter, reading the newspaper in the beach house. "Merry Christmas," Tang said, opening the cupboard and taking down two mugs.

Annoyance bristled up her spine. Jade looked so comfortable, as if she belonged here. And today, of all days, Tang did not. She rubbed the sleep from her eyes and leaned against the counter, waiting for the last drops of percolating coffee to dribble and hiss into the pot.

The floorboards creaked, and Nolan strode into the kitchen, humming "White Christmas." He swept past her, grabbed a mug, and lifted the pot from the coffeemaker, sliding his mug underneath to catch the brown stream. When he was finished, he replaced the pot and strolled out of the room without a *good morning* or *merry Christmas*.

Only a few more days. Then, the invaders would leave. If the meteorologist hadn't predicted record-breaking snowstorms over the Christmas holiday in Vermont, then Layla wouldn't have invited her family to the beach house. They would have flown to Vermont, like they had for Thanksgiving, and been home before the new year.

The coffee sputtered to a stop, and Tang poured a mugful for Jade and set it on the counter along with a small container of half-and-half and a bowl of sugar.

"Thank you, dear." Jade fixed the coffee the way she liked it and sipped, turning the page to the comics.

"You're welcome."

Tang poured a second mug and carried it down the hallway to the master bedroom, where Layla slept, curled on her side, a fist tucked underneath her chin. No remnants remained of their most recent fight, yelling in whispers in the walk-in pantry, Layla complaining about Tang's dour mood and Tang blaming Layla's family for her foulness. Lately, they couldn't get along, it seemed. Everything brushed the other the wrong way. Maybe it was the stress of the holiday season, the foggy days and dreary nights, the loneliness of no family for Tang, the claustrophobia of too much family for Layla. Whatever the reason, a fissure had developed in their relationship, a miniscule hairline fracture.

Layla always said, "See, good thing we aren't married. If we broke up, it'd be much easier than divorce."

And Tang always responded, "If we were married, we wouldn't be fighting. We'd be on the same team."

But would they? An ache greater than annoyance lodged in Tang's sour stomach, and she set the mug on the nightstand and kissed Layla's forehead.

"Merry Christmas," she whispered, then left the room.

On her way back to the kitchen, she paused beneath the threshold of the sunroom. Nolan had plugged in the lights of the Christmas tree, and the spectacle of rainbow colors and glittering tinsel filled the largest room in the house with a warm and comforting glow. She breathed in and smiled for a moment until she noticed Nolan sitting on the sofa, flipping through one of her notebooks lying on the coffee table before setting it aside and returning to humming a song.

Anger flared underneath the surface of her skin, but she bit back her sharp words and retreated to the kitchen.

"My family is nosy," Layla had warned. "Put everything away you don't want them to touch."

Tang stopped from a tirade of self-reprimand and poured herself a mug of coffee and a splash of vanilla creamer instead.

On the counter, her cell phone pinged. Each night, she left it there to charge. After grabbing the phone, she tapped her four-digit passcode, then swiped the screen to examine the message from Dee.

—Merry Christmas! Wish I were with you!—

A puddle of warmth bathed her. After weeks of daily texts and emails and video chats and promises of another visit—soon, always soon—Tang clung to the hope of a future with Dee. Layla, once her first choice, had receded into the distance, more a nagging roommate than a romantic friend. At one point, Dee had hinted at flying to San Francisco for the holidays, but her brother had recommended escaping to the warmth and sunshine of Florida. Photos of beaches and sunsets dazzled her texts. This text included a selfie of Dee posing in a red-and-white bikini beside a Christmas tree.

Smiling, Tang typed her response.

—Miss you too! Merry Christmas!—

Tang added a bunch of hugging and kissing emojis before she unplugged the phone and tucked it into the pocket of her robe.

"Was that your family, dear?" Jade asked.

Tang brought the mug of sweetened coffee to her lips and breathed in the aroma. Hadn't she told them her adoptive parents had died years ago, leaving her with relatives who had never cared about her existence, often whispering behind her parents' backs about the slant-eyed, yellow-skinned foreigner in their midst? But no one knew about Dee—her muse, her desire, her secret—and the hidden privacy of this knowledge kept her safe when threatened by the nosy nature of Layla's family.

"Yes," she lied. "That's a distant cousin in China, wishing me a merry Christmas."

Jade smiled, setting aside the paper and patting the stool beside her. "Tell me about your family, dear. What are the Chinese like?"

Taking a seat, Tang cradled the mug against her chin and dreamed up an imaginary family, full of everything she had ever wanted.

***

After dinner, Layla, Nolan, Jade, and Tang opened their gifts beside the Christmas tree in the sunroom. They huddled together, bundled up in sweaters, with the heat turned up. Mugs of eggnog and apple cider were clustered around discarded wrapping paper and ribbon on the coffee table. Christmas carols floated from the stereo speakers. Nolan sang along with every tune. Jade sometimes accompanied him. Layla only smiled, and Tang observed.

Outside, the bay roiled with high tide. A few miles north, the predicted Pacific Ocean storm crushed waves along the jagged coast. Rainfall splattered against the windows, and Tang glanced up, feeling like a statue in the middle of a snow globe, protected from the elements, safely contained within the glitter and glow of the glass-domed room.

A ring from down the hallway pierced the music.

Tang stiffened her shoulders and stood, placing her mug of cider on the coffee table. "I'll get it." The jolt of the sound had jump-started her lulling heartbeat into a faster rhythm, and she strode down the hallway toward the master bedroom, anxious to stop the insistent noise from the landline. She didn't bother flicking on the light since she figured it must be an automated spam caller.

After yanking the receiver from the phone, she placed the mouthpiece near her chin and said, "Hello?"

"Tang. Merry Christmas." Dee's voice, light and lilting, floated into the room.

"How did you get this number?" The anxiety shifted into fear, and she gripped the receiver tight against her ear and padded toward the doorway. She glimpsed the light spilling into the hallway from the sunroom, where laughter and music and rainfall echoed.

"I needed to hear your voice," Dee said. "I needed to know what you would do to me if I were with you right now, wearing nothing."

"It must be after midnight in Florida," Tang said. "Shouldn't you be sleeping?"

"I can't sleep. I keep thinking of you in the last house we saw." She sighed, her breath deepening. "You're pushed up against the counter, your skirt is bunched up against your waist, and your legs are parted." She lowered her voice. "Tell me what you would have done if it had been me standing there."

Tang tugged the sweater against her heated skin and stepped away from the doorway. She loosened her grip on the phone and pressed her back against the wall. The rainfall pattered against the roof, and the shadow of tree branches whipped across the bed. A fierce wind howled. She swallowed, blinked. No longer in the bedroom she shared with Layla, but kneeling in the fifth house, her fingers damp with moisture, the secret scent of Dee filling her senses like a heady perfume.

"I would …" she began, telling in exquisite detail every movement of her lips, her tongue, her fingers.

She listened to Dee's reactions, the hitch of her breath, the sudden burst of words—*oh, yes*, and *I'm coming*.

"Tang, who is it?" Layla's voice barreled down the hallway.

"I have to go." With trembling fingers, Tang dropped the phone into the cradle.

She stalked on wobbly legs into the cheery sunroom. Her gaze swept across the room, touching on Nolan's wide mouth singing "Silent Night" and Jade's swaying body and Layla's curious and insistent stare that bordered on a glower.

A reflective impulse kicked into gear, and Tang flashed a false smile. "Wrong number," she said.

Chapter Twenty-Two

TANG
Present Day
Bodega Bay, California

Who had written about endings not being happy because you could only be happy if things had not ended? Was it the poet Donald Hall? Or had it been someone else, someone more recent? Tang couldn't remember.

She stared at the open manuscript on her laptop, the cursor blinking where she had left off, the story dangling by the final scene. The scene she'd imagined Dee would help her finish the last time they spoke and touched. The gaping abyss, where happiness had been, now promised nothing but emptiness.

After taking a deep breath, Tang closed her eyes, fingers poised over the keys. The rush of the ocean behind her, the warmth of the sun beating through the windows, the clock ticking against the wall, the hollowness of the house nothing more than a shell against the elements. Layla would be home in four hours. She expected a finished story. Even Ken had sent an email, asking for a status update.

I can't keep the editors waiting much longer, he had written. *Some of them think this whole story is a hoax since I've been chatting about it for months with nothing to show.*

Opening her eyes, Tang reread the paragraphs leading up to the restaurant scene.

Marcus reached across the table and grasped Ya's hand.

Tang imagined what Dee might have suggested Marcus say. *"Will you marry me?" He opened a tiny box, revealing a family heirloom ring of black onyx set in sterling silver.*

As Tang wrote, tears welled up behind her eyes.

"How can I marry you when I'm living with someone else?"

She blinked, and tears spilled down her cheeks. She sobbed.

"Leave her. Move to New York."

She stopped typing, then pressed the backspace, erasing the words Ya had not said.

More tears streamed down Tang's cheeks. Why hadn't she left Layla and moved to New York? What had stopped her?

Breathing, she wiped her moist cheeks with the back of her hand and continued typing the final scene.

"Will you marry me?" Marcus asked, opening a tiny blue box.

Ya gaped at the diamond solitaire.

A faint voice whispered in her ear, "He is a good man, from a good family. He will take care of you."

Ya stared at the ring, as if hypnotized by the glitter of the diamond and the words of the mysterious voice she sometimes heard. After a long moment, she nodded. "Yes, I'll marry you."

Marcus smiled, sliding the ring on her finger. "I will love you forever."

Tang typed *The End* and saved the document.

Before she could think about anything, she opened her email, attached the document, and sent it to Ken with a brief note: *Sorry it took so long. Thank you for your patience. Please let me know how the submission goes. Sincerely, Tang.*

She turned off the laptop, stood, and arched her back. Then, she padded over to the windows, the sun blaring through the glass. The promised heatwave resulted in droves of people flocking to the beach, their colorful clothes and umbrellas like confetti on the sand.

Finding her phone on the coffee table, she stalked into the kitchen and typed a message to Layla.

—*Story done and sent to the agent. Let's celebrate. I'll cook something special.*—

From the refrigerator, she poured a glass of cucumber-infused water and sat on a stool to drink the crisp, refreshing coolness. Memories bubbled up, and she tamped them down, filling her mind with what to make for dinner. Something light, so she wouldn't have to use the stove. A salad or a cold dish. Maybe balela or tabbouleh. No. Layla wasn't a fan of Mediterranean food.

Tang tapped her chin, thinking. A nectarine summer salad. Hadn't Layla picked up some fruit from the farmers market? Tang checked the woven basket. Nothing.

She opened the pantry and sorted through the cans, then glanced at the shelves in the refrigerator. She had the ingredients for gazpacho. If she started now, the soup would be chilled in time for dinner.

***

"Excellent dinner." Layla washed the bowls and wiped them dry, stacking them in the cupboard.

"I'm glad you liked it." Tang smiled, leaning against the counter.

The sun had set, and the heat had calmed. The tourists gone and the roads quiet. A light breeze floated through the partially opened window.

"May I read the ending?" Layla dried her hands and hung the towel on the rack. A curious glint in her green eyes.

Tang shrugged. What harm would reading do? "Sure. I'll bring out my laptop."

"No, let's go sit together." Layla grabbed her hand and led her to the sunroom.

Tang turned on the laptop and curled her feet underneath her hips on the sofa. She brought up the document and scrolled down to the last chapter. "Here." She handed the laptop to Layla.

Hunched over the computer, Layla enlarged the print and read. Her eyes tracked the words, one line after another. The intent expression on her face hardened, then softened, then hardened again. When she was finished, she set the laptop on the coffee table and sank against the cushions. "I don't know why it took you so long to finish. The ending is simple. Just like I suggested. And I'm not a writer."

Nodding, Tang uncurled her legs and scooted to the edge of the sofa. She closed the document and turned off the laptop,

83

snapping it shut and returning it to her desk. What would she work on now that the story was finished?

"And your agent thinks he can sell the book for thousands of dollars?" Layla frowned, the lines around her mouth puckering.

"He thinks the ancestral ghosts add a unique aspect to the otherwise standard trope of arranged marriages." The rote answer slipped off her tongue effortlessly.

"I don't know." Layla stared at the view of the bay and beyond through the windows. "I've read a lot of your short stories, and I think those are better." She glanced at Tang. "Something is missing."

Tang met her gaze and held it for a long moment. What harm would there be in telling Layla the truth now that Dee was gone?

"Well … the original story didn't end with a happily ever after. But I changed it because romance must end with happiness or it's not a romance."

"How did the original story end?" Layla leaned forward and furrowed her brow.

Standing, Tang paced. Her memories drifted back to that night, the last night she had seen Dee. The sudden ring of Dee's phone shattering the silence. The boy's photograph smiling up at them from the phone's wallpaper. The hushed whispers of reassurance.

"Sweetheart."
"Who is he?"
"That's Tyler, my nephew."
"He looks just like you."
The kernel of doubt planted.
"I don't want children." Tang removed the ring, set it on the coffee table. *"I can't marry you."*
"He's my nephew. I hardly see him," Dee pleaded, picking up the ring and holding it out like a promise.
"What else aren't you telling me?"
"I don't know what you're talking about."

"Yes, you do." Doubt spread, a wild vine. *"Now, tell me or leave."*

"Tang?" Layla stood, grabbing her elbow. "Sit, please, and tell me."

Bowing her head, Tang sighed. "I shouldn't."

"Why not?" Layla's voice softened, her grip slipping from her elbow. "You tell me everything."

Tang bit her lower lip and clenched her hands into fists. *I used to. Before Dee. How can I go back and tell you everything I've kept hidden without fracturing the foundation of our relationship?* "Marcus dies."

"Why?" Layla gasped. "He's healthy in the story. What went wrong?"

"Ya killed him."

"She what?"

Nodding, Tang repeated, "She killed him. Because she couldn't marry a man she didn't know."

Layla sank back on the sofa, patting the space beside her. "This story is more interesting than the one you've written."

"But the story I wrote will sell." Tang sat and crossed her ankles and folded her hands in her lap. "The one I just told you would sit on my hard drive forever."

Thinking, Layla shook her head. "You could rewrite it as a mystery instead of a romance."

"But I already sent the story to Ken. He's submitting it to publishers."

"Tomorrow is Friday. You can intercept him." Layla stood and retrieved the laptop. "Send him an email tonight. He'll get it in the morning."

Tang laughed bitterly. *Tell him to call off the sale? So I can write the story as it happened, one word at a time, through Marcus and Ya, instead of Dee and myself? Impossible.*

Layla opened the laptop and the email program. "Here. I'll wait."

Tang stared at the inbox. She had received an email from Ken. Should she open it? Or ignore it?

"What's taking you so long?" Layla asked.

Swallowing, Tang swiveled the computer, so Layla could see. "Ken already responded to my previous email." She clicked on the message.

Tang, thanks for sending this along. Well worth the wait. My favorite editor has made a preemptive offer. I tried calling, but you didn't answer. Please respond ASAP. I think you should take it. Avoid an auction. Those things don't always end well despite what you read in Publishers Weekly.

"What does that mean?" Layla asked.

The pulse beat in Tang's fingertips, pushing the blood back into her brain until her head throbbed with pain. "It means … the book has sold."

Chapter Twenty-Three

TANG
Six Months Ago
Bodega Bay, California

Ring, ring, ring.

Tang lurched off the sofa and darted down the hallway to the bedroom, her pulse pounding in her chest. *Dee.*

She had spoken with her since the holidays—often and not enough—between the bustle of everyday living. Dee often hanging up abruptly. Tang, dazed and confused by the sudden silence.

Suddenly, Dee had warned her against sending gifts, explicit text messages, and lengthy emails. "You can say whatever you want to me over the phone, but don't say anything important anywhere else."

Tang had thought Dee was concerned about Layla, fearful of the consequences of exposure.

She grabbed the phone and breathed, "Hello?" before glancing at the caller ID on the answering machine.

"Tang, it's Nolan. Is Layla around?"

"Yes, just a moment." Breathless, Tang laid the receiver on the nightstand and wandered down the hallway, calling for Layla. "It's your brother. It sounds important."

Layla dropped the newspaper on the floor of the sunroom and stood, shoving her reading glasses to the top of her head. "Mother," she whispered.

Wide-eyed, Tang watched her stagger down the hallway and shut the bedroom door. Tang slipped into the sunroom, picked up and folded the newspaper, and placed it on the coffee table. Sinking into the sofa cushions, she stared out the windows at the sullen sky and gray water and waited.

A few minutes later, Layla returned, misty-eyed. "We have to go to Vermont." Her voice quavered. "Nolan thinks Mom's dying."

Tang scooted to the edge of the sofa and held her breath. "What did the doctor say?"

Shaking her head, Layla swallowed. "Who cares what the doctor said? She's old. I must see her." Her voice broke. "I didn't get to say good-bye to my dad. I want to say good-bye to my mom."

A stab of jealousy pierced Tang's chest. She hadn't had a choice when her parents passed. By the time she had received the call about the accident, her parents had been loaded in an ambulance, headed for the emergency room. They were both pronounced dead upon arrival. Tang met the coroner and identified the bodies. She asked about the details. The police report stated a hit-and-run. Her father had been driving, his car idling in the intersection during a routine left turn at a signal light. From the opposite direction, a van had barreled through the red light and T-boned the vehicle. Bent steel and shattered fiberglass and exploded air bags and blood everywhere. When Tang traveled to the scene, the debris had already been swept up and disposed. Only bloodstains on the pavement had remained, a Rorschach test of disaster.

"Okay. I'll come with you," Tang said. "I'll have Aaron watch my business." Residential real estate on the coast was always slow during the winter months, and Tang did not expect things to be any different this year.

The day before they flew to Vermont, Tang met Bert at Doran Regional Park for a three-mile run. At the end of the beach, where the sand disappeared between the bay and a steep cliff, he stopped and removed a faded paperback book from his pocket. The frayed edges were water-stained and curled, but the spine was sturdy and the pages intact.

"For you to borrow," he said. "Maybe it'll help."

Panting, Tang flipped through the rippled and highlighted pages, her eyes registering random words. *The Tibetan Book of the Dead. The bardo of dying. The process of rebirth. The invocations.*

Frowning, she held up the volume. "What is this?"

Huffing, he jabbed his fists against his hips and gulped mouthfuls of air into his lungs. "It's my version of a bible," he said. "Open the front cover."

Tang obeyed.

Glancing over the top of her head, he read the handwritten verse.

When the appearances of this life dissolve,
May I with ease and great happiness,
Let go of all attachments to this life,
Like a child returning home.

He nodded toward the book. "I read that chant over and over when I suspect a person is dying. I don't know if it helps them, but it calms me." He shrugged. "Maybe it will work for Layla's mom or you or Layla or her brother."

Bowing her head, she ran her finger over the loopy scrawl of Bert's handwriting. The words seemed to imprint a feeling of comfort through her skin, and she smiled, closing the book and pressing it against her chest. "Thank you."

He waved a hand, brushing away the comment. "You'd do the same for me."

And though Tang had never thought about it, she knew he was right.

The next day, during the early morning flight to Burlington, Tang removed the book from her backpack and opened the front cover, whispering the verse over and over again until she memorized the words.

Layla glanced away from the window and narrowed her gaze. "What are you reading?"

"*The Tibetan Book of the Dead*," Tang said, showing her the cover of a Buddha sitting cross-legged on a cushion. "I'm borrowing it from Bert. He thought it might bring comfort to your mother."

Sighing, Layla shook her head. "Bert doesn't know my mother's a Christian. She's not some New Age born-again hippie from Woodstock."

A jolt of fear rippled up Tang's back, and she closed the book and shoved it into her backpack. "I don't think he meant to offend you or your mother."

"Of course not," Layla said. "He's Bert. He doesn't mean to hurt anyone." She frowned, jutting her chin toward the backpack. "Promise me you won't show that book to my mother."

Tang thought about the verse she had memorized, the only thing Bert had said she needed to know. She would recite it, if needed, and she would not tell Layla's mother where she had learned the words. "I promise."

***

Johnson, Vermont

As Tang strode against the wind toward the bank of taxis idling along the curb of the arrivals area of the Burlington International Airport, blustering snow flurries bombarded her. The late afternoon sun glinted off the snowbanks, and Tang wished she had remembered her sunglasses.

With a raised arm, Layla caught the attention of a driver.

He popped the trunk and grabbed the two suitcases with his gloved hands.

Layla opened the back door and motioned for Tang to slide across the cracked leather seat that smelled of perspiration and disinfectant.

As soon as she was seated, Tang banged her mittened hands together, trying to spark warmth.

The driver bounded into the front seat, turned up the heat, and glanced in the rearview mirror. "Where to?"

"Johnson," Layla said, rattling off the address to the maple farm.

"I know that place," the driver said, pulling into traffic. "My niece loves the maple sugar cookies shaped like leaves. I buy her a full box each Christmas." He squinted into the rearview mirror. "You tourists?"

"Family," Layla said, removing her gloves and scrolling through her phone to text her brother about their arrival. "We're here to visit my mother. She's sick."

Tang watched the driver's face change from courteous to intrigued.

"Oh, you're Mrs. Goodfellow's daughter. The one who moved to California to repair the shores."

Wincing, Tang snuck a glance at Layla, who hated when people misinterpreted her job. Layla didn't repair shorelines. She designed revetments, bulkheads, and seawalls to stabilize shoreland properties against erosion.

But Layla didn't look offended. She lowered the phone and met the driver's gaze in the rearview mirror and smiled. "Yes, that's me."

"Your mother's very proud of you," he said, stopping at a light. "She said you're the only one in the family who was smart enough to escape the hardships of a Vermont winter." He shook his head, turning onto the highway. "She's right, you know. This year's shaping up to be a record-breaker."

Layla reached for Tang's mittened hand. "I'm thankful for many things. Including living in California," she said.

Tang met her loving gaze and squeezed her hand. "Me too," she said.

***

The taxi inched through streets slick with ice and slush. The Gihon river was partially frozen. A blizzard of flakes fell like a flapping white sheet across the windshield.

The driveway leading to the farm was covered with snow.

The driver parked on the street and removed their suitcases. "Do you need help?" He nodded toward the gray mounds covering the path.

"No, I think we've got it," Layla said, handing Tang a suitcase.

Tang gripped the handle through her mitten and squinted against a gust of flurries. The bitter wind chapped her face and

91

stung her eyes. Following Layla, she trekked up the buried walkway. Each step in her boots sank deeper and deeper until Tang thought her thighs might be damp. By the time she made it to the front door, her face was numb, and snot from her runny nose had dried into a frozen trail from nostril to lip.

Shivering, Layla knocked on the door and rang the doorbell.

Within moments, Nolan pulled back the door and grabbed their suitcases.

Following Layla's example, Tang rubbed the soles of her boots against the scrubber before stepping into the foyer. The blast of warm air thawed her face, and her nose started to run again. Quickly, she shed her mittens, coat, and boots. Rubbing her hands together, she trailed after Nolan and Layla toward the family room and the fireplace.

"How's Mom?" Layla asked.

"Sleeping." Nolan handed them each a mug of cider. "I'll put these suitcases in your old bedroom. You two thaw off, and then we'll see if Mom's awake."

Layla grabbed a tissue from the coffee table and handed it to Tang before she sank into the nearest sofa and stretched out her legs.

After Tang rubbed her nose dry, she sat next to Layla and let the steaming sweet cider warm her face. The gold-and-crimson flames crackled and popped in a hypnotic dance inside the fireplace. Tang stared, lulled into a trance, broken only by the insistent ring of her cell phone from inside her purse.

Glaring, Layla nodded to the offending noise.

"Maybe it's Aaron." Tang set the mug on a coaster on the coffee table and rummaged in her purse for her phone. Glancing at the screen, she cringed and panicked. *Dee*. Hadn't she already warned her not to call or text for the next two weeks? With her heartbeat thundering against her ribs, she swiped the call to voice mail. "Spam."

A hardness tightened the muscles in Layla's jaw. "I thought the Do Not Call Registry would take care of those pesky telemarketers, but I was wrong." She shook her head, gazing at the fire. "There's always a way around the rules, pretending you're doing market research or with a nonprofit or a political campaign. When the truth is, you're selling something."

Tang's phone beeped with a message.

Layla jutted her chin toward the phone in Tang's hand. "I bet that's an automated message."

Suddenly, the phone felt unbearably hot.

Tang dropped it back into her purse. "I don't need to listen to it."

"You might as well put it on speaker, so we both can laugh at the robotic voice."

"Maybe later." Tang picked up the mug and took a sip of the cider, savoring the notes of apple juice, cinnamon, and maple syrup on her tongue.

Layla dived her hand into the purse. "Why not now? We need some entertainment."

"No." Tang lurched for the phone.

But Layla grabbed it first, but the phone was locked. "When did you put a passcode on your phone?" She narrowed her gaze.

"Just recently. For work." Tang clutched the mug tighter, her pulse hammering against her skull.

"Unlock it. I want to listen to the message." Layla held out the phone.

Tang held her breath. Fear stiffened her spine and froze her shoulders.

"Fine. I'll guess." Layla jabbed a series of numbers on the keypad.

Tang watched.

Within moments, Layla had guessed the passcode. She swiped the screen and pressed play on the message.

Tang held her breath, waiting for the worst to happen.

Dee's voice rang out into the room, as if she had stepped inside from the cold.

"Hey, it's me. Your little Dee-Dee. Why don't you come and visit? You're so close. You could rent a car and be here in seven hours with traffic and the storm. Call me."

Layla shifted on the sofa, squaring her hips toward Tang. "Who's Dee-Dee?"

Swallowing, Tang stared at the phone in Layla's hand. From experience, she knew lies were easiest to tell people who wanted to believe you, and lies were always easiest to remember when they were closest to the truth. "She's a client. The one I met in October. She lives in New York City. I told her I would be away from the office for two weeks, and she must have assumed I would be available for a brief visit since I didn't tell her the reason why I'm here."

"Why would she want you to visit?" Layla furrowed her brow.

"Because we've become friends." The words sounded hollow and empty, even when Tang tried to infuse them with levity and warmth.

"Friends?" Layla turned the phone over in her hand. "You don't usually befriend your clients."

"I know." Tang took another sip of cider, biding time. "She's different. You'd like her."

"Why haven't you mentioned her before if she's a friend?"

"Because I was waiting to introduce you in person the next time she comes out."

"And when is that going to be?"

"Soon." Tang stared at the phone and sighed. How many times had she begged Dee to fly out again? "She's busy. She's in sales, and her work sends her all over the country. Every time I've tried to schedule a follow-up appointment, she ends up canceling at the last minute."

Layla shook the phone. "Why did she call herself *your* little Dee-Dee?"

Knots tightened in Tang's lower back. She placed the mug on the coffee table. "She's just being playful and funny."

The floorboards creaked, and Nolan's shadow fell between them. "Mom's awake. Who wants to see her first?"

Layla stood, a towering pillar of anger. She aimed the phone at Tang's chest. "You'd better not be cheating on me."

"I'm not." Tang felt the lie roll around like a marble in her mouth.

She outstretched her hand, palm up, and wiggled her fingers for her phone. But a part of her didn't care if Layla scrolled through the call logs and text messages. She kept everything from every client. And Dee was a client. That much was true.

"We're not finished." Layla tucked the phone into her back pocket and stalked out of the room.

Tang felt the heat of Layla's fury blaze through her. She tucked her hand into her lap, dropped her chin toward her chest, and stared at her feet. Worry twisted around her ankles and wove around her legs, cinching into a knot around her stomach.

Nolan heaved a sigh and sank into the recliner. "You two having problems?"

Glancing up, Tang noticed his posture. He leaned forward, hands clasped, ready to listen. But Tang didn't know if she could trust him.

"Doesn't every relationship have problems?"

"Not every relationship. Mom and Dad got along."

"Then, why aren't you married?"

He chuckled, releasing his hands and leaning back into the recliner.

Tang couldn't find the humor in the question. She shifted her focus to the guilt lodged in her stomach and remembered something Bert had once attributed to Buddha: *You can't hide the moon, the sun, and the truth for long.* She rubbed her hands over her face. Would the truth finally come out?

***

After Tang brushed her teeth and dressed in pajamas, she met Layla in the bedroom. Without a word, Tang climbed into the double bed and turned off the light. She had not spoken with Layla since the voice mail message from Dee earlier in the day. The seven hours of travel, the gravity of Jade's illness, and the strain of secrets weighed heavily on her as she closed her eyes and tried to sleep.

Layla leaned over and kissed her cheek. "Good night."

"Good night," Tang whispered without opening her eyes.

In the darkness, a melody jangled.

Tang stiffened, and her hands clenched against her chest.

"It's her," Layla said, rolling over on her side. "Answer it."

Sitting, Tang reached for the phone on the nightstand and swiped the green button across the screen. "Hello?"

"Can you talk?" Dee asked, breathless. "I miss you."

Tang shot a sidelong glance at Layla's curved body. She looked so vulnerable, like a child, curled up, hurting, and alone.

A twinge of guilt overwhelmed the dullness of desire, and Tang whispered, "I can't be your friend, Dee." She swallowed, her chest tightening. "You also need to find another real estate agent. I'm out of the office, but I will refer you to someone else when I get back."

"Layla knows," Dee whispered. "Who told her?"

"Please, don't call me again." Tang pressed the red button and placed the phone facedown on the nightstand. Something inside of her severed—something once vital and alive, now dead and gone.

"You didn't have to be so dramatic," Layla said.

Tang slipped beneath the covers and clasped her hands against the thumping heartbeat in her chest. "I felt like I had to choose between her and you, so I chose you."

Turning, Layla touched her shoulder. "You didn't have to choose."

"So, we can all be friends?" The venom in her voice stung. Tang lurched and grabbed the phone, tossing it on the bed. "Then, call her back. Explain the rules."

"Don't be so defensive." Layla sat, nodding to the phone. "I just wanted to know what she meant to you—that's all."

"She means nothing, okay?"

"Then, why are you yelling?"

"I'm not yelling."

"You could have fooled me." Huffing, Layla turned on the lamp beside her. A puddle of light pooled on the bed.

Tang blinked back the pressure in her eyes and swallowed the tightness in her throat. "I'll stick to having male friends. No complications."

"She wasn't a friend."

"Then, what was she?" Glowering, Tang pushed aside the mountain of comforter and sheets. Anger coursed through her, boiling her blood. "Whatever she was, she isn't anymore. So, let's drop it and go to bed."

"No, let's not drop anything." Layla punched a fist into the sheets. "You were having an affair." Her voice broke with tears. "You were cheating on me."

Affair. Cheating. The words slapped against Tang's ears, stinging parts of her she hadn't known she had. She clenched her teeth, grinding the molars. Lies had gotten her here. Lies would get her out.

"How could I cheat on you with a straight woman? She has a boyfriend, who's ready to propose to her any day. And a son. She just likes to flirt and tease. Don't you have friends who flirt and tease each other?"

Shaking her head, Layla scoffed. "My friends take each other seriously."

Too seriously. Tang thought of Robin's intellectual discourse and Bert's solemn diatribes on compassion. Why did everything have to be serious?

Bowing her head, Layla rubbed her hand against the sheets. "I can't imagine someone else kissing you."

"Then, don't." Tang pushed her hair off her forehead and sighed. She swept her arms open, encompassing the room. "I'm not driving to New York City to be with another woman. I'm here, with you." She patted Layla's hand.

Lifting her chin, Layla met her gaze. "I don't want to lose you."

Those misty sea-green eyes punctured Tang's heart. She squeezed Layla's fingers, pressing warmth back into them. "You haven't lost me," Tang said, her heartbeat fluttering in her chest. *I almost lost you.*

A week of silence followed.

Silence from Dee.

Silence from Layla.

Silence from Nolan.

Only Jade wanted to talk.

"Come here, dear." Jade patted the space beside her on the white sheets. "I have something to ask you."

Tang cringed, fearing the worst—deathbed promises she couldn't keep. But she padded across the bedroom and sank onto the mattress. Jade smelled sickly sweet and fermented, like rotted fruit. Outside, the snowstorm had finally ended. Sunlight, deceptively bright but cold, glinted through the lace curtains in the window. Even with two layers of clothes, Tang shivered.

Jade lay on the white bed, surrounded by white pillows, her white hair a tangled cloud. Her breath a rasp. From underneath the covers, she lifted a hand.

"Yes?" Tang touched Jade's cool, translucent skin, the veins like blue rivers on a map, thick and twisted, running everywhere. She bent from her waist until her ear was parallel to Jade's mouth and waited.

"Will you take care of Layla and Nolan when I'm gone?"

Take care of them. "How?" Tang had never been asked to take care of anyone.

Blinking, Jade squeezed her hand. "Make sure they stay in touch, get together for the holidays, and love one another."

"Why me?"

"Because you're not obligated to be here. You understand love is a choice. I want you to remind them to choose each other." She jiggled her hand. "Can you do that for me, dear?"

Tang held her breath against the stench of death and nodded.

Clutching her hand tighter, Jade lifted her head and widened her eyes. "One more thing." She paused to gather her strength. "You don't have to be who you think you are." She coughed and released Tang's hand. Closing her eyes, Jade breathed, a whistle of air and water. "You don't have to be who you think you are." She whispered the sentence like a mantra—its meaning opaque and hidden, a puzzle to be solved.

Tang stood. An eerie feeling surrounded her. She almost expected to see a veil lift, revealing a glimpse of another world. But the room remained intact, a blinding nebulous of white.

Slowly, she wandered into the dark hallway, her feet soft and quiet against the hardwood floor. She found Layla and Nolan in the family room. They looked like two strangers sitting on a bench, waiting for a train to take them away from here. No wonder Jade was concerned.

Glancing from one to the other, Tang said, "I think she's ready to go."

One by one, they filed back into the white bedroom.

When the appearances of this life dissolve ...

Jade lay on her back, her hands resting at her sides, the pauses between each breath growing longer and longer.

May I with ease and great happiness ...

Gasping, Layla covered her face with her hands and buried her head against Tang's shoulder. A ragged sob shook her body.

Let go of all attachments to this life ...

Nolan bowed his head and closed his eyes.

Like a child returning home.

As softly as a kiss, Jade sighed and breathed no more. Her presence left the room.

Tang pressed Layla closer and rubbed her back, blotting out the distance.

Chapter Twenty-Four

TANG
Present Day
Bodega Bay, California

"I talked to Ken." Tang poured a cup of coffee for Layla and handed it to her.

"And?" Layla took a sip.

Turning toward the kitchen window, Tang watched the sun struggle over the horizon. The sky was clear, no fog, the beginnings of another hot day. "He doesn't like the alternative ending. He suggested I take the offer on the table."

"For how much?"

Tang winced, knowing Layla's practical nature wouldn't understand the realities of the publishing industry. And with Dee's death, Tang really wanted Layla's approval.

She glanced over her shoulder. "I don't want your criticism or judgment. I already feel like a failure."

"Oh, sweetheart, I could never do what you do. Make up things out of thin air." With one hand, Layla twirled her fingers up like smoke. "How could you believe I would even think that?"

"Because you've been at your wits' end with this whole process."

"Okay, you're right." Layla cupped the mug with both hands. "I'm a little testy." A flint of something—jealousy or anger—drifted over her face, then fell into hardness. "But you can't blame the way I feel. This book has consumed your life for the past two years." Layla set the mug on the counter and stood by Tang's side. "I just want you back." She wrapped an arm around Tang's shoulders and tugged her close. "I'm being selfish."

Leaning against the warmth radiating from Layla's skin, Tang took a deep breath. "I could earn more, selling a house."

Layla tightened her hold. "Don't take the offer." Scowling, she dropped her arm and stepped aside. "That book is worth so much more, and you know it."

Did she? Just last night, Layla had questioned the novel's worth, not believing it would sell in the thousands. She was right. It had not. But Tang didn't want to say any more. She just braced her arms against the sink and returned her gaze to the sunrise.

Layla crossed her arms over her chest and broadened her stance. "Withdraw the book. Rewrite the story. You don't have to sell for next to nothing."

Biting her lower lip, Tang heaved a sigh. "I thought about that option."

The conversation with Ken had lasted only ten minutes, but during that time, every possibility had been discussed.

A wave of fear crashed through her, and she considered lying to make Layla happy. But something Jade had said on her deathbed returned to Tang, and she reconsidered.

"I decided to follow Ken's advice and take the offer." She sniffed back the tears threatening to crest in her eyes. The bay and the ocean beyond shimmered like a bowl of light. "Please, don't judge me." She paused, regaining her strength. "I don't want to be one of those writers who spends their entire life perfecting a masterpiece that never sells."

She thought of Van Gogh and his brother supporting him and how she had resolved early on that she would never be like him. Any offer was better than no offer at this point, especially with Dee gone. Tang's breath hitched as she remembered the soothing words Dee had spoken to reassure her, keep her going, even though, in retrospect, everything Dee had ever said to her was a spoke in a wheel of lies.

Sighing, Layla took a step forward and cupped Tang's shoulders. "I'm sorry I sound angry." She massaged her fingers through the fabric of Tang's robe. "I'm just frustrated for you. Two years, and the amount you're earning is less than minimum wage."

"Well, the saying that writing is a labor of love is true." Tang closed her eyes and sighed, relaxing into the movement of Layla's fingers kneading the knots out of her muscles. "I'm just glad the book is done and sold." She opened her eyes, staring at the floor. "This chapter of my life is over. I can begin something else."

After dropping her hands from Tang's shoulders, Layla wrapped her arms around Tang's waist and pulled her close. The seams of their bodies blurred into one. "You're right. We can both start over. Plan our trip to Europe. Enjoy retirement."

Tang laughed. "*You* can enjoy retirement. I'm still working."

Layla kissed the top of Tang's head. "Sell your business to Aaron. Retire with me." She lowered her voice to a whisper. "I want to enjoy each moment with you again. Just like in the beginning."

In the beginning ... Tang blinked, remembering the slide of earth beneath her business shoes when she had trailed after Layla toward the landslide.

"Stay back," Layla had warned. "I don't want you to get hurt."

But that's what love does to us, doesn't it? Tang thought. *It opens us up, exposing all our vulnerabilities, which means we're never safe, which means we can always be hurt.*

Chapter Twenty-Five

DEE
Five Months Ago
Upper West Side, New York City, New York

"Why didn't you stop by when you were in Vermont?" I asked over the phone. "I know Layla suspected something, but you could have denied it."

"Is that why you keep calling from a restricted number?" Tang hissed.

I clutched a hand to my chest, glancing at the time on the stove. Ryan and Tyler would be returning from a play date in a few minutes. "That's the only way you'll pick up my calls."

"I shouldn't be talking with you."

"I thought you loved me." Anger flared my nostrils.

Should, should not—I was frustrated with all the damn rules and regulations that made up Tang's life because Layla couldn't share like a normal adult. Like Ryan. He didn't care about the broad strokes or the details. I could have my second life and the first one too. Why couldn't Tang?

"Even if Layla hadn't suspected anything, I wouldn't have come over," Tang said, her voice rising. "Don't you know it's rude to leave someone who's dying?"

"She wasn't even your mother," I said, tapping my foot against the linoleum. Four minutes.

Tang sighed. "I can't do this anymore."

"Do what?" I demanded.

"Love two people at the same time."

I snorted, tossing back my blonde hair. "Loving as many people as possible is easy. Your heart grows and makes space." Bile rose in my throat. "Or is yours stunted?"

"Okay. Stop with the insults. Or I won't come out and visit you in a few weeks."

Was she still considering this possibility even though she just said she couldn't do this anymore? I paced back and forth across the tile floor. Or was she just saying what I wanted to hear? I stopped moving and stared at a spot on the kitchen counter. My heartbeat ticked in my chest. "You'll visit?"

"Yes, I'll fly out. Just be nice to me."

A key jangled in the lock.

"Great. I've got to go. Text me the details."

I ended the call and slid the warm phone into a pocket and arranged a smile on my face. "You guys are early." I opened a cabinet and pulled out a pot, placing it on the stove. "I thought I'd make dinner tonight."

Ryan chuckled, taking the pot off the stove. He kissed my mouth and slipped a hand underneath my shirt, brushing his fingertips across a nipple.

I groaned, arching closer.

"I left Tyler at his friend's house. We'll pick him up after dinner." He nibbled my throat.

Mmm. I slumped against him. My mind drifted, and his roaming hands and mouth transformed into Tang's small fingers and delicate tongue. Yes, oh, yes. I wanted Tang to touch me. Touch me like *this*.

Chapter Twenty-Six

TANG
Five Months Ago
Bodega Bay, California

Tang ended the call with Dee and sank back in her office chair, her gaze fixed on a spot in the parking lot. She had combed through the calendar, trying to find a space available for a quick trip to New York City, but she had to maneuver between Aaron's needs and Layla's insecurities.

Three raps on the door, followed by Aaron striding into the office. He was a short, trim man with a mess of black hair over his slanted eyes. Originally from Korea, he spoke perfect English without an accent and had the best penmanship of anyone Tang knew. He also dressed impeccably in button-down shirts and slacks, answered all calls professionally, and kept abreast of the housing inventory. But he was young, only thirty, and lacked the social acumen Tang had developed over the years.

"How may I help you?" Tang folded her hands on the desk.

"I've brought copies of the five listings I showed your buyers this morning." Aaron set a file folder on the desk and took a seat across from her. "They're in the conference room, ready to write an offer on the home in Occidental."

"Excellent." Tang smiled and picked up the folder, flipping through its contents. "Would you like to write the offer?"

"Really?" Wide-eyed, he leaned forward.

"Yes, I could use the help." Tang had always supervised Aaron, never letting him go alone to showings or listings until she left with Layla to care for Jade. But if she wanted to go to New York, she would have to entrust Aaron with more responsibility and make it worth his time and effort. "I'll give you a raise and a thirty percent share in my commissions."

Gasping, he leaped to his feet. "Thank you."

"You're welcome." She handed him the file and broadened her smile. "You deserve it, Aaron."

After he left and closed the door, Tang returned to studying the calendar, wondering if she should really take that trip to New York City or if she should just let go of Dee.

Chapter Twenty-Seven

TANG
Five Months Ago
Bodega Bay, California

"Is business still slow?" Layla asked, plugging Tang's phone into the charger.

Every night, while Tang cooked dinner, Layla scrolled through Tang's phone, which was no longer locked. After dinner, Layla searched the browsing history on Tang's computer and read through all the emails. Tang would answer any questions Layla might have, and if satisfied, the evening would end with a sense of complete openness and intimacy, not quite as exciting as the early days of passion, but not nearly as raw and painful as those first few weeks after Dee's voice mail in Vermont.

"It's starting to pick up," Tang said, seasoning the chicken before placing it in the oven and setting the timer for forty-five minutes.

She didn't worry anymore what Layla might find on her phone or her computer now that Dee no longer contacted her at home.

A sense of calm restored her confidence, and she pushed back her shoulders, turning toward Layla. "How was your day?"

Layla shrugged, picking up the teakettle from the stove and pouring more hot water into her mug of herbal tea. "I can't complain. The soil samples came back from that stretch of highway just north of us." She paused, and the lines around her lips puckered. "That road will collapse in ten years if we don't do something." She took a sip and stared at the carrots Tang was chopping on the cutting board. "I'm working on a proposal to redirect the road three hundred yards to the east to bypass any danger. I figure it will be the cheaper solution."

"Do you think the county will approve your proposal?"

Layla leaned against the counter and crossed her ankles, hugging the mug of tea to her chest. "If they don't, they'll spend an exorbitant amount of money trying to remedy the situation after the road has collapsed and lives are lost."

"Always preventive, aren't you?" Tang slid the chopped carrots into a mixing bowl already filled with onions and garlic and cauliflower. She sidestepped around Layla and rinsed the cutting board and knife in the sink.

A trilling melody played from Tang's phone.

Layla set aside her mug and unplugged the phone from the charger. "Restricted number," she said before swiping her finger across the screen. "Hello?"

Dee.

Tang dropped the cutting board into the sink. It clattered, and water splashed. Her heartbeat jackhammered in her chest, and her knees wobbled. She turned off the faucet and dried her hands, waiting for their life to collapse.

For a long moment, Layla stood silently with the phone pressed against her ear. Then, she lowered the phone and stared at the screen. "I thought I heard some noise in the background before the call ended, but I can't be sure." She frowned, plugging the phone back into the charger. "I hate telemarketers."

"Me too," Tang's voice squeaked. She would not go to New York City. Not now. Not ever. "That's why I let those calls go to voice mail," she said. "They usually hang up if I don't answer."

"Good idea," Layla said, picking up her mug. "I shouldn't be so paranoid anymore, but I am sometimes." She glanced over at Tang and smiled. "I just don't want anything bad to happen to us."

"It won't." Tang met her gaze and returned her smile, but her heart pounded, and her legs trembled.

Tomorrow, she would stop taking Dee's calls. And just to be certain, she would also instruct Aaron to not answer any calls from a restricted number. No need to invite trouble where there was none.

Chapter Twenty-Eight

DEE
Four Months Ago
Chicago, Illinois

I can't believe Tang won't pick up when I call from a restricted number. I tugged my luggage across the airport, searching for the terminal for the flight to JFK. Sleep fogged my mind, but my body powered forward, breaking up clusters of people. *How can I plan for her trip to New York City if I can't talk to her?* A flare of anger seized my chest. *Maybe she changed her mind, and there is no trip.* I scanned the signs, pausing in front of the line of passengers getting ready to board. *I bet she canceled it because of backward-thinking Layla.*

Fumbling in my purse, I removed my phone and placed it under the scanner.

"Thank you, Ms. James," the boarding attendant said. "Have a good flight."

"I will."

As soon as the plane's Wi-Fi became available, I planned on answering emails. I tossed the phone back into my purse and stalked across the jetway.

If Tang wouldn't come out to New York, then I would have to come to California. I would not let too much time pass between us.

Chapter Twenty-Nine

TANG
Present Day
Bodega Bay, California

"Congratulations, Tang." Bert folded her to his chest. "Layla told us the good news about the book."

"Thanks." Tang smiled, turning her head so the side of her face rested against his scratchy shirt.

"Now, the hard part comes," Robin said, patting her shoulder. "All those rewrites the editor requires before the book is published." He held up a bottle of champagne. "But tonight, we celebrate!"

Layla wandered into the foyer. "We're on the deck tonight." She took the bottle of champagne and waved them into the hallway. "Tang, bring the glasses."

Tang wiggled out of Bert's arms, gathered four flutes from the kitchen, and strolled out through the sunroom onto the deck. She set the glasses on the picnic table and squinted at the sunlight on the water below. Heat singed the air. From the beach, the ruckus of people playing and laughing and talking sounded like background music.

Robin placed a floppy hat on his head and slid a pair of sunglasses up the bridge of his nose and stood by the railing, surveying the crowds. He looked more like a tourist on a cruise ship than a retired college professor. "See the fog coming in." He pointed toward the horizon. "I don't remember how long it's been since I've looked forward to seeing its presence."

"I didn't mind the warm days," Tang said. "Except I had to get up earlier for my runs."

Layla nodded, uncorking the champagne. "And I could have done without the traffic."

"Agreed." Tang brought a glass of champagne to Bert and another one to Robin. She returned to Layla's side. "One night, you didn't get home until after seven. I thought something bad had happened."

Smiling, Layla pulled her close and kissed the top of her head. "Oh, baby, you worry too much."

Robin chuckled, lifting his glass. "To Tang! May her book be a bestseller!"

"To Tang!" Bert clicked his glass to theirs.

Tang took a sip of the dry, bubbly sweetness. "I like writing, but it also feels good to say I've written something."

Bert took a seat at the picnic table and curled his shoulders toward his chest. He looked like a quarterback resting on the bench. He was quiet—quieter than usual.

After scooting next to him, Tang rubbed his arm. "Are you okay?"

With a sidelong glance, he nodded. "I'm just glad no wind came with this heat. We don't need another wildfire." He huffed, staring out at the two seagulls perched on the railing. "My bones still remember that call last year from Mendocino County. Nineteen days without a break. And the entire fire took almost a month to contain."

Tang nodded, thinking back on the heatwave that had driven thousands of people to the coast, causing traffic jams and parking nightmares. Strangers had even traipsed through their side yard to the steps leading to the beach.

"I'm glad Layla built a barricade after I found a family inching their way through our property when I took out the trash."

"No use in calling the sheriff," Robin said, refilling his glass. "They were all too busy issuing parking tickets or turning people away from the crowded beaches."

Tang slid out from the bench, her stomach grumbling. "Well, I'm hungry. Anyone interested in helping me bring out the goodies?"

"I'll help." Bert stood, arching his back. "I need the exercise."

"Don't forget the plates," Layla said, sinking into a lounge chair.

Inside, the stuffy sunroom felt like a petri dish beneath a microscope, exposed and subject to unwanted attention. Tang had already closed the blinds and pulled the curtains in the rooms facing the side yard and the street, hoping to avoid a glimpse of yet another stranger peering into the windows, curiosity intersecting with a sudden lack of privacy. In the kitchen, she pulled out a tray of assorted cheeses and cold cuts and a tray of sliced carrots, broccoli, and celery sticks, surrounding a bread bowl of spinach dip, and handed them to Bert. She shut the refrigerator door with her hip and grabbed a stack of plates and napkins from the old oak cabinets.

"I wanted to talk to you away from the others," Bert said.

Tang clutched the plates and napkins. She didn't like the way Bert was fidgeting, shifting his stance from foot to foot, a worried crease lining his forehead. "Yes?"

"Remember that accident last week?"

Nodding, Tang sucked in a breath. Her body stilled. *Now what?*

"We recovered the woman's phone. We thought it was dead, but we charged it." Bert lowered his voice. "You sent a text message after the crash, asking if she was okay."

Perspiration dotted Tang's forehead. She tightened her sweaty grip on the plates, the napkins sliding dangerously near the edge.

"You knew the woman," Bert said. "I thought you were just being curious when you asked about the crash last week. But you weren't." He took a step closer, his body filling the doorway. "You knew her." He narrowed his gaze. "Why didn't you say something?"

Thinking, Tang took a step back. She didn't want to hurt Layla, especially now that everything was back on track with the book completed and plans for a long-awaited trip underway. "I didn't know until *after* I talked with you."

"When you found out, why didn't you tell me?" Bert inched closer, curling his big body down toward hers.

She shrugged. "What could you have done?"

Bert sagged his shoulders, the trays still in his hands. "I could have told the family I knew you."

Shaking her head, Tang swallowed against the pressure in her throat, the same pressure that built up against the backs of her eyes. "It's best you didn't know." She bowed her head. "Her brother told me not to contact them." After lifting her head, she met his gaze. "I never should have become involved with her."

"Why did you?" Bert frowned.

Tang blinked, glancing up at the ceiling. "She was my muse. She inspired the book I just sold."

Bert nodded, his frown deepening. "Does Layla know?"

"Layla knows I ended things six months ago." Tang studied Bert with a sidelong glance. "I would appreciate you not mentioning what you told me."

"Will you tell her?" His voice sounded painfully soft.

Tang felt the phantom limbs of guilt curl around her body, squeezing until the air expelled, and she gasped. "It's over. She's dead. Why not let sleeping dogs lie?"

Bert shook his head. "Because these dogs are *not* sleeping."

Chapter Thirty

TANG
Three Months Ago
Bodega Bay, California

"Get rid of her," Tang ordered Aaron.

She leaned forward in the office chair and slammed a fist against the desk. Anger pulsed beneath her skin. How dare Dee contact her assistant under the guise of buying real estate? Didn't she know how precious time was when running your own business? She and Aaron didn't have the luxury to research homes for someone who wasn't interested in buying. But how could she disclose this information to Aaron without revealing the truth of her relationship with Dee?

Tang exhaled and leaned back in her office chair, the air-conditioning vent shoving cold air on her head. She shuddered. Time to approach the problem from a different angle.

"Tell her she's unrealistic, wanting to buy beachfront property for under a million dollars."

Aaron loomed over the desk, waving a file folder. "She says she inherited a lot of cash and wants to invest in a fixer-upper off the coast."

Tang laughed. How stupid did Dee think she was? "Tell her to provide proof of funds." She organized the printout of listings on her desk, shuffling through her thoughts—wondering how this faux buying proposition, created to hide the real reason for seeing each other, would evolve into something tangible and out of control.

Frowning, she glanced up and met Aaron's heated gaze. "I thought I told you in March to refer her to another agent."

Aaron stepped back, a sheepish expression flitting across his face. "I ... I didn't want ... to ... to lose the sale," he stammered, "so I've kept in touch."

A jolt of surprise startled Tang. *Why didn't I take care of the situation when I returned from Vermont? Then, I wouldn't be dealing with any of these problems in the height of the selling season.* Pressure built against her temples, and she rubbed her forehead. *Why didn't I tell Dee over the phone that I never wanted to talk to her again?* Worry thumped against her ribs, and anxiety chilled the back of her neck. *Why did I rely on the slow fade?*

Since that strategy hadn't work, she shifted her approach, leveling a gaze at Aaron. "What did I tell you about the rules of real estate sales?"

Aaron tipped back his head and gazed at the ceiling. "Always dump a client if they don't make an offer after four weeks or after viewing ten homes." He lowered his gaze and added, "Whichever comes first." Shaking the file in his hand, he took a step forward. "But you only showed her five homes. And her circumstances have changed. Surely, those conditions restart the clock." He sighed, lowering the file to his side. "Doesn't she deserve another chance?"

I can't believe I'm having this conversation. Tang bowed her head, rubbing the sore spot where a headache had bloomed. "I'm busy with serious clients. I don't need the hassle."

"Then, let me handle her," Aaron pleaded, sinking into the chair facing the desk. "I promise I'll stop pursuing the sale if she doesn't make an offer when she comes out for her next visit."

What next visit? A spike of fear zipped through her system, jump-starting another round of panic. Lifting her head and narrowing her eyes, Tang struggled to modulate her voice. "When is she coming out?"

"August."

Three months away. Tang scrubbed her face with her hands, smearing mascara down her cheeks. Weeks ago, she had stopped taking Dee's calls from a restricted number. Didn't the woman know the relationship was over? Tang slowed her breath, her body chilled. Apparently not.

"I want you to stop talking with her." When Tang registered the resistance in Aaron's posture, she straightened her spine and gritted her teeth. "I've been in this business long enough to know she's a looky-loo. Believe me, she'll never buy."

Aaron shoved back the chair and stood, clutching the file in his fist. "Let me get that proof of funds from the bank. Then, I'll decide."

"No." Tang slapped the desk, standing. "I'm still your boss." She thumbed her chest. "I refuse to let you pursue this client." Her voice rose to a dangerous pitch. She strode across the room and shut the door for a bit of privacy. She took a deep breath, trying to cool the boiling frustration from Aaron's pushback. "Drop her." She tilted back her head to meet his gaze. Every muscle in her body vibrated like a plucked string. "Or I'll fire you."

"If you drop the client and fire me, then may I go on my own with her?" A vein in his neck quivered. "She swears she can spend up to two million dollars." His voice broke. "My wife is pregnant. We need the money."

Tang shook her head, clenching and unclenching her fists. "Money isn't everything. Haven't you learned that by now?" She strode to her seat by the window overlooking the parking lot and spun to face him. "I can list off all those problem clients who weren't worth the commission." She lifted her hand, curling back each finger as she spoke. "Hardies, Steele, Greenberg—"

"Okay." Aaron raised his arms, the file flapping in his hand like a flag of surrender. "I see your point. I don't agree with it, but I see it."

"Drop her," Tang repeated.

Aaron sagged his shoulders. "She doesn't sound difficult."

Tang sank into her chair, leaning back until the pressure in her neck released. "Trust me," she whispered. "She. Is. Very. Difficult."

Without a word, Aaron swiveled on his heels, opened the door, and left.

Silence rang like a bell.

Sounds of office life floated into the room—the chatter of gossip, the ring of telephones, the clip of heels along the

116

walkways, the click and hum of the copier and the printer, the *glug, glug, glug* of the bottled water dispenser.

A knot tightened in her stomach. Where would she find another assistant as good as Aaron? Worry washed over her. She stood and strode across the room and shut the door. *I hope he listens*. She pressed her back against the hollow wood separating her from the rest of the office. Closing her eyes, she listened to the steady rhythm of her heart. *I don't want to have to fire him. But if he keeps talking with Dee, I will.*

***

That night, Tang curled up next to Layla in bed and nudged her shoulder. "You up?"

"Mmm … yes." Layla turned to face her in the dark.

Through the filmy curtains, the moonlight illuminated the hollows of her cheeks, the glint of mischief in her eyes. In the distance, the sound of waves crashing on the beach rumbled like a lullaby. Tang fumbled for Layla's hand beneath the sheets and found her skin warm and leathery, the pads of her fingers callous from digging into the earth.

Fear clawed into Tang's throat, and she swallowed. "I have a problem at work."

As Layla shifted against the pillow, the spark in her eyes dimmed to seriousness. "What's wrong?" She wrapped her other arm around Tang's shoulder.

"Aaron never referred Dee to another real estate agent." Tang heaved a sigh. "He's been talking to her and sending her listings." Biting her lip, she tried to steady the panic building in her chest. "I told him if he doesn't stop talking to her, I would have to fire him. I don't want her causing problems for us anymore."

"Oh, baby." Layla tugged her hand free and brushed Tang's face, wiping away the tears spilling down her cheeks and soaking into the pillow. "I wouldn't worry. Let Aaron handle her. He needs the responsibility." She kissed her damp mouth. "And you need more time to write, so you can finish that story you promised your agent."

Confusion knotted Tang's thoughts. "But I thought you didn't want me talking with her."

"You're not. *He* is." Layla stroked her hair and pulled her close.

Tang smelled the scent of Layla's lavender soap in the crook of her arm, remembering the last time—which had also been the first time—she had lain beside Dee, breathing in the scent of her skin and the sweetness of her touch. Oh, how so much had changed over the months—the attraction building into hope and love and pleasure before sliding into fear and panic and darkness. She wiggled until she found Layla's lips and kissed her until she could taste the salty tears mingled with their love, her lips swollen with passion. She did not want to lose this woman who had been her rock, even in the shadowy depths of temptation.

Breaking away, she gasped, "I'm scared."

"Of what?" Layla frowned, the skin between her eyebrows pinched.

"Of Dee." Tang rolled onto her back and stared at the ceiling, the tears dried on her cheeks and chin.

"She can't hurt us." Layla's hand found her fingers. "If you have to help Aaron represent her, then I trust you'll do the right thing."

"I'm not like you." Tang shook her head, remembering the guilt beneath her skin. "I haven't always done the right thing."

"That was then," Layla said, closing the distance between them. "This is now."

Tang closed her eyes, feeling Layla's lips move down her body.

Jade's last words surfaced in her mind. *"You don't have to be who you think you are."*

But how do I become someone else?

Chapter Thirty-One

TANG
Present Day
Bodega Bay, California

"I don't know what you're talking about." Tang clutched the napkins and plates in her sweaty hands, her heartbeat ratcheting in her chest.

Bert loomed in the kitchen doorway, blocking an escape to the deck to join the others. "The toxicology report showed abnormally high levels of alcohol in her blood." He frowned, balancing the trays of food in his hands. "The investigators think she fell asleep at the wheel. The skid marks on the street suggest she woke up long enough to brake, but not on time." He broadened his stance. "Is that what happened?"

"Why ask me?" Tang widened her eyes, her thoughts racing.

"Because I think you know the truth."

Footsteps creaked against the wooden floor.

"Do you guys need help?" Layla's voice floated down the hallway.

Bert shifted out of the doorway and flashed a smile. "We're coming."

Layla wedged into the kitchen, glancing from Bert to Tang. "Is everything all right?" She touched Tang's shoulder. "You look a little pale."

Nodding, Tang avoided Layla's gaze and followed Bert out of the room. Outside, the heat crashed into her. She stumbled toward the picnic table, placing the plates on top of the napkins. A breeze ruffled the ends of her hair. She panned her gaze across the deck and settled on the fog rolling across the horizon, promising to blanket everything in a heavy mist.

"Are you sure you're all right?" Layla grazed her hand across Tang's hip. "You and Bert seem a little tense."

Tang glanced over her shoulder at Bert, who had slumped into the lounge chair next to Robin, who chattered on and on about something. Would he tell Layla about that night if she didn't? As if sensing something, Bert swung his gaze in her direction. The dark eyes smoldered. Tang sucked in her breath and spun her head toward the beach.

Without glancing at Layla who stood beside her, Tang said, "After everyone leaves tonight, I have something to tell you."

"Why can't you tell me now?" Layla shifted closer, sealing the gap between them. Bending from the waist, she stretched her arms out against the railing. "I'm listening."

Tang exhaled her breath and swiveled away. "Not here, not now."

Turning, Layla stepped away. "I'll get the cards and chips. We can play while we eat."

The shuffle of Layla's feet receded, followed by the click of the French doors.

A set of heavier feet stomped across the deck.

Tang glanced up at Bert, who had joined her at the railing. "Don't worry," Tang said. "I'm telling her tonight."

"How much?" Bert asked.

The creases in his forehead matched the fear in her chest. What did she have to lose? "Everything," Tang said.

***

In the kitchen, long after Bert and Robin left, Tang finished loading the dishwasher. She plugged her cell phone into the charger and turned off the light.

In the master bedroom, she found Layla propped against the pillows, watching the news on TV. A slight breeze drifted into the room from the partially opened window. The flutter of white curtains reminded Tang of the long, flowing dress she had tried on during the retirement sale at Brides 'n Maids. She bit her lip, stanching the memory of the days when she had dreamed of

120

marrying Layla. Now, years later, she wondered if her dream of marriage had more to do with the idea than the person. She brushed her teeth and scrubbed her face clean, the hot water and soap massaging deep into her pores. She stared at her reflection—the eyes dark and narrow, the small nose, the slash of lips. Some people would rather die than tell the truth. Tang was not one of them.

Stepping out into the bedroom, she stood before Layla and waited.

Layla turned off the TV. "You look like you're about to witness an execution."

Nodding, Tang circled the bed, stripped her clothes, and slid under the covers.

Layla turned off the light and scooted across the mattress.

Tang laced her fingers through Layla's warm hand.

"What do you have to tell me?" Layla asked.

After taking a deep breath, Tang began.

Chapter Thirty-Two

TANG
August 6th
Bodega Bay, California

"Aaron, slow down." Tang held the cell phone against her ear, straining to hear above the crash of the waves.

She padded across the deck and slipped into the sunroom, shutting the French doors behind her. The noonday sun beat through the glass enclosure, heating the room like the inside of an oven.

Tang stalked past her open laptop on the coffee table, the final chapter of her novel halfway written, the ten-minute break to watch the water cut short by Aaron's phone call. "What's wrong?"

"My wife's sick. I need to take her to the emergency room. The baby—" He broke into a sob.

"Shh, shh," Tang whispered. "It's all right. What do you have planned today?"

"Just the open house. I canceled everything else this morning. I thought my wife might be better by then, but she's not." He gasped. "I just need you to cover the open house."

Good thing I didn't go with Layla to Vermont. Tang sank into the sofa cushions and grabbed her notebook, turning to a fresh page. With her pen poised, she asked, "Which property?"

"Salmon Creek." He slowed his breath. "The horse property."

She scribbled down the address. "One to four, correct?"

"Yes. The signs are at the office."

Tang slid her finger back and forth across the mouse pad to glimpse the time in the lower-right corner of the laptop. Twelve fifteen. She'd better dress and leave now if she wanted to be there before the public milled around the property, searching for the agent.

"No worries. I'll take care of it. You go take care of your wife … and the baby." Oh, how she hoped his wife didn't lose the baby.

"I will," Aaron said. "Thank you. I'll text you with updates."

"Please do." Tang ended the call.

She saved her work and shut off the computer. She would have to finish the final chapter after the open house and before Layla came home.

Chapter Thirty-Three

TANG
Present Day
Bodega Bay, California

"Why are you telling me this now?" Layla asked.

Tang rolled over onto her back, staring at the ceiling. "Because it's important. Not the fact that Aaron's wife was sick—thankfully, she's better now, and so is the baby—but what came later." She took a deep breath, exhaled, and squeezed Layla's hand. "When I went to the office to pick up the open house signs, I didn't see the white truck in the parking lot. Or if I did, I didn't think it belonged to anyone I knew. But she was there, waiting."

"Who was there?" Layla's voice sounded faint, far away.

"Dee." The syllable slipped out of Tang's mouth like the fourth letter of the alphabet, a child's voice, innocent and full of wonder. "She had an appointment to see property with Aaron that morning. He canceled. She came anyway."

"Why would she do that?" Layla asked.

Tang swallowed. Shadows danced on the ceiling from the moonlight spilling through the swaying branches. "I don't know."

Chapter Thirty-Four

TANG
August 6th
Bodega Bay, California

Tang closed and locked the front door of the Salmon Creek property. She slipped the keys into the lockbox and gathered her purse and guest book, full of new real estate leads. The sun was still warm, but the breeze had picked up. The cool, briny scent wafted across her face, strands of hair blowing into her eyes.

She unlocked the doors, tossed her purse and guest book on the passenger seat, and popped the trunk. Her black flats scrunched to the end of the driveway. She folded the sign and carried it back to the car, slipping it into the trunk. Only two more signs to collect—one by the end of the street and another by the three-way stop.

Before leaving the property, Tang sent a text to Aaron.

—Open house a success. I'll leave the guest book on your desk, so you can follow up tomorrow. How is your wife and baby?—

No response.

No surprise. The reception on the bay was spotty, at best. She called the office phone and left a message with the same information. Aaron didn't have a landline. Most people didn't, or if they did, they never shared it with anyone.

Checking the time, Tang debated on whether to return the open house signs to the office or just drive home. After all, she planned on being back at work tomorrow. She had taken the week off to finish the book. If she skipped the office, she would save a half hour. More time to write. She had promised Layla she would have the book completed. But Tang also had the guest book to drop off. Aaron came into work earlier than she did. He could follow up on the leads, assuming everything was all right with his

125

expectant wife. Holding on to the guest book until tomorrow made no logical sense. She would go to the office, take the extra time, leave nothing unfinished.

Again, she didn't notice the white truck following her on Highway 1. She didn't pay attention until she pulled into the office parking lot. Only two other cars were parked by the building—both coworkers, who were probably dropping off their open house gear for the night. She glimpsed the white truck on the street, circling past the building, disappearing behind a grove of eucalyptus trees, the medicinal scent heavy in the air. But she didn't think it was Dee.

She only thought, *How strange*, when the truck rounded the street again, like a horse on a carousel.

On the drive home, Tang decided to stop by the deli to pick up dinner. Between the heat and the deadline, she didn't want to cook. The parking lot was full, as always, and she had to wait for a spot to open. Two cars idled behind her, but she ignored them. After grabbing her purse, she trudged through the gravel lot and swung open the glass door, a swoosh of air-conditioning blasting her warm face. She stepped up to the deli counter and smiled at Farim, the son of the owner, who took her order for a pepperoni pizza. While waiting, she grabbed a six-pack of beer and a bag of locally baked chocolate chip cookies—Layla's favorite—and paid at the register. By the time she finished shopping, the pizza was ready.

Outside, the sun had dipped lower.

She unlocked the car and placed the pizza, beer, and cookies on the passenger seat. As she pulled out of the lot, she glanced in the rearview mirror and noticed the same white truck pulling out of a spot.

A prickle of fear inched across her scalp. *Am I being followed?*

She pulled out onto the highway, the two-lane road winding up along the coast. Every now and then, she glanced into the rearview mirror. But the truck was gone.

Breathing a bit easier, she chided herself. *Why am I being paranoid? Who would want to follow me? I'm no one.*

By the time she arrived at the cottage overlooking the bay, she had forgotten about the white truck. She pulled into the drive, pushing the button for the one-car garage, and slid into the dark space. After turning off the engine, she stepped out and rounded the vehicle, bending to retrieve the food.

"Do you need help?"

Glancing up too quickly, she bumped her head against the doorframe. She winced, rubbing the top of her head. In the dim light of the garage, she struggled to glimpse the owner of the voice.

The shadowy figure stepped closer. The crunch of gravel against the soles of shoes sounded almost as loud as the ticking of Tang's heart.

Slowly, the figure came into focus.

The long, slim body, like a silver blade. The blonde hair in a high ponytail. The dark eyes and red lips.

Dee Young.

Tang gripped the doorframe, glancing over her shoulder. But there was only one way out of the garage to get to the house or the street—passing Dee. Once Tang had stopped taking the restricted phone calls, she had assumed the relationship was over and she would never see Dee again.

But here she was, standing in the opening of the one-car garage, her arms outstretched, ready. "Do you need help with our dinner?" she asked.

Our dinner?

Tang felt her mouth dry. Her voice lodged somewhere deep in her throat. Every muscle in her body stiffened.

"Didn't Aaron tell you I would be coming out?" Dee took a step closer and lowered her arms. "Aren't you happy to see me?"

The memories flooded back. Lies. Secrecy. Stolen kisses. Forbidden sex. The guilt, once dormant, rose again.

What to do? What to do? Never in her life had Tang wished more for Layla to be here at this moment, in the house, rushing out to greet her, to save her from whatever was about to occur.

Chapter Thirty-Five

TANG
Present Day
Bodega Bay, California

Layla gasped, clutching Tang's hand tighter. "Dee followed you home?"

Nodding, Tang squeezed Layla's fingers. "I'm sorry." Her voice broke, more a croak than a whisper. She should have told Layla immediately when she came home. It was the right thing to do. Guilt dug its nails into her legs. She squirmed. Oh, why had she neglected to do the right thing? Would she always be who she thought she was—a liar, an adulteress?

The air stilled. The curtains settled. The shadows lingered on the ceiling.

Layla rustled, shifting from her side onto her back, then onto her side again. "And you swear you didn't know she was following you?"

Tang rubbed her head up and down against the soft pillow. "I noticed the truck several times, but I didn't think it was Dee's brother's truck. I had only seen it once before, when she came out last October to view property." She cringed. Oh, why had she pretended Dee was a client when she was someone else? She heaved a sigh, deciding the previous deception was too much to dismantle. "I just wanted to get home, eat dinner, and finish the book before you arrived."

Layla released Tang's hand. "You told me you didn't finish the book that night."

Tang winced at Layla's cold, hard, unyielding voice. Why did Layla doubt the truth? Tang tightened with protest.

"That's right. I didn't finish the book. I wrote that alternative ending I told you about."

"Where Ya kills Marcus?"

"Yes."

Layla snapped on the light, obliterating the shadows. "Where is this story going?" A frown creased her forehead and tugged at the edges of her lips.

Squinting from the bright light, Tang opened her mouth, but her throat closed. After clawing into a sitting position, she grasped the bottle of water on the nightstand and unscrewed the cap and took a long swallow. When she was finished, she wiped her moist lips with the back of her hand. Glancing over at Layla's tense body, Tang wished she could go back ten days or fourteen months, whichever point in time she needed to return to erase everything that threatened to destroy them.

Chapter Thirty-Six

TANG
August 6th
Bodega Bay, California

"Of course I'm happy to see you," Tang lied. "I'm just surprised."

"You don't look surprised." Squinting, Dee pushed the strap of her black leather purse high against her shoulder and took a step forward. "You look scared, almost terrified."

Of course I'm scared. I haven't seen you for months, and you show up, uninvited, at my home. Why wouldn't I be scared?

Tang smiled and grabbed the food from the passenger seat and shut the door with her hip. "Aaron didn't tell me you were coming."

"He's not the best assistant, is he?" Dee grabbed the beer and cookies off the pizza box and followed Tang to the side door of the faded blue shingled house. "I always imagined your home would be bigger and with a view."

"The view's inside." Tang spun, clicking the garage door opener on her keychain before unlocking the side door. She felt Dee shadowing her, the heat from her body radiating like a direct flame. If Dee stepped too close, Tang would catch fire. "I usually bring guests through the front door into the foyer. This laundry room entry isn't impressive."

Tang stepped into the narrow space, the washer and dryer on one side, the folding table on the other, a swinging door straight ahead. She glanced over her shoulder, like she would if she were showing this property to a potential buyer. But Dee wasn't a buyer. She was a former lover, padding across the linoleum, a six-pack of beer in one hand, a bag of freshly baked chocolate chip cookies in the other, her gaze sweeping across the room, her blonde ponytail swinging like a horse's tail.

Tang faced forward and pressed a hand against the swinging door into the kitchen.

"Oh, wow. Now, this is impressive," Dee said, setting the beer and cookies on the quartz counter, her lips agape, her eyes wide in exaggerated *o*'s. "This kitchen is almost as big as my apartment in New York City." She circled the stovetop island and barstools and stepped toward the sink with the window overlooking the bay. "Is this where you call me?"

I don't call you anymore. Tang placed the pizza next to the beer and cookies and removed plates from the old oak cabinet. "The reception is best right where you're standing." *Next to the knives and the chopping block and the gun I wish I had right about now.*

Dee unzipped her purse and removed her cell phone. Leaning over the sink, she took a snapshot of the view. The white tank top she wore rode up above the waist of her faded denim jeans, exposing the tender flesh.

Tang glanced away, avoiding temptation. "There's a better view from the deck off the sunroom." She placed two slices of the pepperoni pizza and one cookie on each plate and searched for the bottle opener.

"Oh, I don't drink beer." Dee tucked her phone into her purse. "Do you have any wine?"

Yes, but she would not serve her the best wine, the wine she reserved for Layla. "You like white or red?"

"White."

Nodding, Tang removed a bottle of Chardonnay from the wine cooler beside the dishwasher. She uncorked the bottle and poured two glasses. "Let's eat on the deck. I'll give you a sweater to borrow. The fog is coming in early."

She motioned for Dee to grab the plates while she carried the wineglasses down the hallway to the sunroom. The glass enclosure glowed like the inside of a light bulb, the room ablaze with the reds, oranges, and golds of the setting sun.

Dee gasped, her gaze taking in the space. "This is where you write."

Nodding, Tang unlocked the French doors and stepped onto the breezy deck. She placed the glasses on the picnic table and returned to the sunroom to grab her tattered sweater off the back of her chair.

After setting the plates beside the wineglasses and her purse on the table, Dee strolled over to the railing and snapped more pictures of the bay leading to the Pacific Ocean.

Once upon a time, Tang imagined having Dee here, on the deck, standing side by side, holding each other. But that time had long passed, after Jade died and the restricted phone calls started. The effort to hide and conceal had competed with the need to expose and reveal everything to Layla to regain her trust. Fear bristled up her back, tensing her shoulders. What would she tell Layla about tonight when she asked how the writing went?

When Tang reached up to drape the sweater across Dee's shoulders, Dee spun and pulled her close, dipping her head and kissing her deeply.

The shock of a foreign tongue in her mouth jolted Tang into a panic, and she pressed the flats of her hands against Dee's chest, shoving her away.

"I thought you liked the way I kiss," Dee said, pouting.

"I did." Tang turned around, walking back toward the house, wondering how she would get Dee to leave. "But I don't anymore."

"Is that why you stopped taking my calls?" Dee strode toward her, her gaze narrowed into tiny slits. "Is that why you gave me to Aaron?"

"I don't like confrontations," Tang said, suddenly aware of the inevitability of having one tonight on the deck while Layla wasn't home. "I didn't want to hurt you."

Dee sucked in a breath and threw open her arms, the sweater spreading across her shoulders like a cape. "I flew out to see you because I love you." She dropped her arms to the sides and paced back and forth across the deck, the heels of her shoes slapping against the stained redwood planks. Pausing, she grabbed a glass of Chardonnay and tipped it back, then drank the second glass, her gaze searching for more.

132

The sky darkened. The food grew cold. The breeze quickened.

"Why don't we go inside and talk?" Tang suggested, picking up the plates.

"Talk about you leaving me?" Dee asked.

"I didn't leave you," Tang said. "We were never together."

Scoffing, Dee shook her head and grabbed her purse and the wineglasses and followed Tang back inside the house. She strode down the hall and into the kitchen, dropping the sweater on the counter and pouring herself another glass of wine. "Where is the lovely Layla anyway?"

Tang stared at the cold, untouched pizza. Oh, how she wished Layla were here right now. She would know how to handle the situation, wouldn't she? "You should go. She's coming back soon."

"How soon?" Dee leaned against the counter, crossing her ankles, and drained another glass of wine.

Glancing at the clock on the stove, Tang registered the time. Eight thirty. "A half hour," she lied.

"That gives us plenty of time to make love," Dee said, emptying the wine bottle.

"I'm on my period." Another lie.

Dee took a sip, a slow smile spreading across her face. "That's fine. You can do all the work this time."

The remnants of guilt clawed at her insides, and Tang stepped farther away, hoping the distance between them would save her.

A phone rang from inside Dee's purse.

Startled, Dee set aside her wineglass and fumbled for the lilting melody.

Tang glimpsed the lock screen. An image of a boy. Blond hair, dark brown eyes. A younger version of Dee.

After swiping her finger across the screen, Dee said, "Hey. Is everything all right? It's way past your bedtime."

Past your bedtime? Tang clenched her jaw.

"I can't right now. I don't have the book." Dee turned away, curling her shoulders. "I'm sorry, sweetheart." Her voice was as soft as a caress.

She's talking to a child.

"When I see you, I'll read to you. Promise. Kissy-kissy, lovey-dovey."

Tang stiffened, fighting against the truth.

"No, I'll talk to him later."

Him? A punch to the gut. *Her brother? Or some other man?*

"Good night."

Everything suddenly clicked into place. *How could I have been so stupid?*

Dee ended the call and tossed the phone back into her purse. She flashed a seductive smile. "Where were we?"

Tang pointed to the purse. "You have a family."

"Of course I do." Dee widened her smile. "My nephew misses me. I promised to read to him when I get back to San Francisco."

"You'd better leave now." Tang nodded toward the clock on the oven. "You don't want him waiting all night."

"We still have a half hour," Dee said, taking a step forward. "I'll go before Layla gets home." She brushed the back of her hand against Tang's cheek.

A slow shiver rippled down Tang's spine. Dee's tangy, sour wine breath filled her nostrils.

How do I get out of this mess?

Chapter Thirty-Seven

TANG
Present Day
Bodega Bay, California

"She was in our house?" Layla's voice rose to a dangerous pitch. "You let her into our house?"

Tang sighed, staring at the ceiling, her hands folded against her chest. "What else was I supposed to do?"

"Call 911," Layla said matter-of-factly. "She was an intruder."

But she was also a former lover, a past friend, a woman deemed safe, not threatening.

"Did she seduce you?" Layla asked. The fear and worry rippled in her voice.

"No," Tang said, the truth somehow harder to speak since she didn't know if Layla would believe her. "She didn't."

"How did you get her to leave?" Layla rolled over and propped her weight onto an elbow.

"Not easily," Tang said.

Chapter Thirty-Eight

TANG
August 6th
Bodega Bay, California

In the kitchen, beneath the overhead lights, Dee rummaged in her purse on the quartz counter and removed a black onyx ring. Dropping to one knee, she grabbed Tang's hand. "Will you marry me?"

Tang gasped. How many times had she asked Layla if they could marry? How many times had Layla said no? Tang stared at the ring, black and fathomless as Dee's eyes, and felt her desire to marry swell against her need to be with the right person.

"Yes, yes, I'll marry you," she said, knowing in her heart that answer was yet another lie.

An insistent trilling sang from Dee's purse.

Dee slid the ring on Tang's finger, then stood and grabbed the phone. Frowning at the caller ID, she asked, "Where's your bathroom?"

Tang pointed to the hallway. "Second door on the right."

"I'll be right back." As Dee strode out of the kitchen, she swiped her finger across the screen and pressed the phone against her ear.

Tang strained to listen.

"Yes, sweetheart." The bathroom door clicked shut, and Dee's voice disappeared behind the blaring noise of the bathroom fan.

Sweetheart. A niggling sense of doubt troubled Tang. *The boy. Is he her nephew or her son?*

Tang waited a moment, her heartbeat thudding in her chest, before she plunged her hand into Dee's purse and removed a black leather wallet. With one snap, she opened the treasure trove and searched the compartments. A New York State driver's license, registered under the name Deidre James. Tang swallowed, her vision blurring. A school photograph of a little boy, the same boy on the lock screen of Dee's phone. With sweaty fingers, Tang turned over the photo. In blue ballpoint ink, a name, an age—Tyler James, eight. Tang gasped. Not Christopher's son. But Dee's son. Who was the father? Tang fanned through the credit cards, all with the name of Deidre James, and stumbled upon an old photograph, bent around the edges, the colors faded, as if bleached by the sun. A platinum blonde in a white gown and veil, wedged against a tall, trim man in a black tuxedo. A red-lipped smile on the woman. Twinkling blue eyes on the man. Tang flipped over the photograph. In blue ballpoint ink, a date—thirteen years ago. The room swayed. Tang's vision blurred, and her throat closed. She fumbled with the evidence, careful to restore everything in its proper place.

After the wallet was nestled inside of the purse, Tang stepped back. She struggled to fill her lungs with air. Quivering, she gripped the ledge of the kitchen sink and gazed out the window. Thick white fog blanketed everything. She could not see beyond the deck. It was as if the moon, the stars, and the water did not exist.

"Sorry that took so long," Dee said, returning to the room. "Is everything okay?"

Tang released her grip on the sink and straightened her spine. "No, it's not."

How could everything be okay when the truth was exposed like a nasty cut spouting blood everywhere? Deidre James, age thirty-nine, had never lost her son in childbirth. He was alive and well. She had just spoken to him on the phone, reassuring him that Mommy would read to him when she returned home.

"I can't marry you." Tang removed the ring and set it on the counter beside the purse. "I don't know who you are."

Dee assumed a pinched expression on her pale face. "I don't understand."

"Who are you?" Tang thumped a fist against the counter. The cold hardness smacked against her knuckles. Blood rushed away from her heart and throbbed in her temples. "Deidre James."

Dee gaped, taking a step closer. "You snooped in my purse." She snatched the bag off the counter.

"You're a stranger." Tang pointed to the back door. "Get out of my house."

"No." Dee closed the gap between them, her body warm. "I won't leave."

Tang spun, seizing a serrated chef's knife from the butcher block by the sink. She wielded the blade, marking the space between them. "Get out now, or I will kill you."

Frowning, Dee skittered away. The door to the laundry room swung back and forth on a squeaky hinge.

Tang plowed forward, the knife leading the way.

The side door banged open, and Dee stumbled down the steps to the white truck. She flung open the driver's door and tossed her purse onto the passenger seat and climbed inside. She slammed the door and revved the engine. Headlights blazed. Tires churned. Gravel sputtered.

Standing in the doorway, Tang gripped the knife. The air swirled around her, thick and cool and moist. But she only felt the blazing heat of anger and deception as she watched the truck speed away, swallowed by the mouth of the fog.

Chapter Thirty-Nine

TANG
Present Day
Bodega Bay, California

Layla gasped. "She's the woman who died in the crash off Hangman's Bend."

Nodding, Tang drew her knees to her chest and wrapped her arms around her calves. From her perch on the mattress, the bedroom looked smaller, no larger than a box or a cage. The air was hot and still, but Tang was too lazy to close the window and turn on the oscillating fan. The memories of that night rushed back into her mind, worn and faded, even in the small lapse of time. The details were blurry, leaving only big shapes and sizes. But the feeling of urgency remained strong.

"I wanted to chase her, drive her off the cliff, but I stayed home."

"Why?" Layla frowned, shifting on her hips, leaning closer.

Tang reached for her hand. "I wanted to be here when you arrived home."

Laughing, Layla squeezed her fingers. "You were asleep when I got home." She released her hand and lowered her voice. "Why didn't you tell me sooner?"

Shrugging, Tang sighed. "I wouldn't have told you at all if Bert hadn't confronted me tonight." She blinked. "He thinks I know what happened, but I only know she left here at a little after eight thirty and crashed around midnight."

"Is there an open investigation?" Layla stood and walked across the room to close the window. She turned on the standing fan. A gush of cool air spun around the room.

Rubbing her bare arms, Tang shook her head. "Bert said the autopsy suggests she fell asleep behind the wheel. The case has been closed as an accident."

"Then, why does Bert care?" Layla hovered by the fan. The air rustled the edges of her nightgown.

She looked like an angel from a tree topper, tall and stately, glowing from within.

Tang smiled sadly, the broken pieces in her settling in place. "I don't know. I guess he was thinking of you."

"Me?" Layla touched her chest.

Nodding, Tang felt the tears building behind her eyes. She knew Bert like she knew her own mind. If she hadn't agreed to share her version of the truth, then he would have. "He wanted you to know."

"Know what?"

"About my affair." Her voice broke. "With a woman I didn't know, a woman who never existed."

Layla crossed over to Tang and took her hands. "You already told me months ago." She sat, and the mattress tilted. "The nightmare is over."

Nodding, Tang released the first round of tears.

Chapter Forty

DEE
August 6th & 7th
Bodega Bay, California

Damn Aaron for canceling our plans.
I can't back out now. I have the truck.
I can't go back home. I need to see Tang.
There is only one thing to do. I drive up north to the coast.

***

Lucky. I'm always lucky. I arrive at the real estate office just as Tang is pulling into the parking lot in her crappy red sedan. But I don't want her to see me. I can't let her see me. I need to take her by surprise, corner her, make her understand she has not won this game of cat and mouse.

So, I circle around the perimeter, dipping low toward the cliffs above the beach, rising high toward the two-lane freeway, until the red car putters toward the main road, going north toward Salmon Creek. I follow, but not too close.

***

I haven't chased a person since college, when the boy I loved fell in love with someone else. He didn't break up with me, but started dating her on the side. The time with me lessened while the time with her increased until there was no time for me at all. For three weeks, I stalked him—classes, dining hall, dorm, dates. I only wanted him to notice me, but I became obscured, a backdrop in his daily drama, nothing but a speck of dust among the trees and buildings and extras that populated our small college town, a town I never think about anymore. And if I no longer think about it, it ceases to exist.

But I want to exist for Tang. I want her to think of me.

I can't bear to be the shadows in her world of sunshine. I need to be the star, the moon, the planets in her universe.

***

She has an open house. From one to four. I have three hours to kill.

I pull out of the gravel driveway and circle back to town. I park on Bodega Highway, outside of the art store and the coffee shop. I buy a soda and a painting for our bathroom. A view of the cliffs and the Pacific Ocean and a halo of black birds circling the sky.

When the time is close, I drive back to the open house and follow her red sedan down the highway to the office, then the deli, and finally to the driveway of her home.

***

"What are you doing here?" Tang asks, circling the vehicle.

The distasteful surprise on her face confuses me. "To see you, of course."

She backs up, glancing over my shoulder. Her gaze sweeps across, searching for an escape. But I know there is nowhere for her to go, but to me.

***

"The best view is from the sunroom," Tang says.

I follow her from the kitchen to the hallway to the sunroom. The burst of light from all the windows. From the deck, I take a picture of the setting sun and send it to Ryan.

—*View from our new home.*—

Within minutes, I receive a text.

—*Great job, sunshine. How much?*—

I type a response, something reasonable and vague.

—*Thirty thousand under asking price. A steal!*—

I don't bother asking about Tyler. It's late in New York. Past his bedtime.

Tang scans the deck, searching, always searching. Doesn't she know I will not leave? I cannot go. Until she tells me why she broke up with me.

"Are you in love with Layla?" I ask.

She doesn't answer, just turns back toward the house.

"Is she better than me?" I question.

Again, she doesn't say anything. She just keeps walking away.

So, I follow her into the kitchen.

"Why did you break up with me?" I wonder.

"If you don't leave, I'll call the police."

"No, you won't." I back her up until she is wedged against the counter by the sink. I crush my mouth against hers.

She squirms for a moment, then relaxes into my arms.

The worry I had ceases. No one who falls under my spell hates me, breaks up with me, leaves me. She is under my spell, hypnotized by my kisses, and I undress her there in the kitchen and make love to her until the outside grows dark and the fog rolls in.

***

An hour later, she takes a seat on a barstool on the counter and eats the cold pizza and drinks the warm beer and nibbles on the hard cookies. She offers me everything. I decline. I have no appetite, except for her.

***

Much later—I don't know how much later—I am sated by her body. And I withdraw the black onyx ring from my purse and ask her to marry me. I want to have everything.

After she says yes, we celebrate with a drink. Wine because there is no champagne. I drink from the bottle, no glass needed. I drink until the bottle is empty. Then, I drink some more.

Sleepy, so sleepy.

"You have to go," Tang says, nudging my shoulder.

I am sitting beside her on the sofa in the sunroom. There are no windows, only white. White fog. Like walls. Enclosing us. I want to sleep.

"Layla will be home soon," she says. "You need to go."

"Come with me," I beg, tugging on her hand, the fingers soft and light like feathers.

"Let me pack," she says.

***

Outside, I start the truck.

She starts the car.

I back up.

She follows.

But I don't know where I'm going. Even with the headlights, I cannot see beyond the hood of the truck's engine. I only know I'm driving through mist.

***

I am driving slowly, so slowly, but the sign warns I am driving too fast.

I brake.

The guardrail bends, then snaps.

And I tumble inside the truck like an amusement park ride, upside down, around and around, until the truck crashes against the rocks, and something catches fire, its red glow burning through the white walls of fog. My head hurts, and I am coughing.

"Tang, Tang, where are you?"

I reach for my purse. But the contents have spilled on the floor, which is now the ceiling, my head upside down, my hair falling in my eyes. My head is ache, ache, aching. So much pain.

Now, smoke mixes with the fog and the flames, and I'm choking. Gasping, coughing, choking, screaming, "Tang! Tang! Tang!"

Chapter Forty-One

TANG
Present Day
Bodega Bay, California

Tang met Bert at Doran Regional Park for an early morning run. The fog curled and dispersed like ribbons off the water, and Tang zipped the jacket up to her chin and plunged her hands into the pockets, bouncing back and forth on the balls of her feet, waiting for Bert to turn off the podcast he had been listening to while waiting for her to arrive.

"I told Layla everything," she said.

Bert nodded, tucking the earbuds and phone in a pocket.

He doesn't believe me.

"We're all right," she said.

Another nod. He started jogging.

Oh no, he wants more. What more can I tell him?

Tang matched his pace—two steps for every one of his. Her feet sank into the moist, dense sand. Her breaths short and even. Her thoughts tucked close, like the movement of her arms beside her body.

He slowed his pace. "Did I tell you what else we found on the phone?"

Did he? "I don't think so." She shortened her stride.

"Photos, timestamped around seven forty-five." He stopped.

"So?" She halted.

"So, everything you say happened checks out about that night." He shot a glance. "But I don't believe you." He tightened his mouth into a grim line. "I'll give you one more chance to tell me."

Tang raised her arms overhead. "Tell you what?" she shouted, and the cry of gulls lifted from the sand. "That I kept her with me for as long as I could?"

He seethed, the air flaring into tiny puff clouds from his nostrils.

She punched a fist into a pocket and withdrew her hand. Uncurling her fingers, she exposed a black-and-silver ring. "*This* is all I have left of her." She thrust it toward his face.

"Layla let you keep the ring?" He nodded to her outstretched palm. "I didn't think she'd allow you to be sentimental."

"You're right. She didn't."

Tang darted toward the waves and threw back her arm, casting the ring through the air. The white surf gulped and swallowed. Panting, she ran back to Bert.

He fixed his gaze on the waves, a deep frown etched on his face. "A love like that never ends."

His large brown eyes held more sorrow than she had ever seen.

I guess that's the end. She stood beside him—a sentinel of grief.

After a long moment, he smiled and nodded toward the end of the beach. "Race you. Last one to the cliffs buys breakfast."

"Deal." Tang bent her knees, ready for the countdown.

"Three, two, one … go!" Bert sprang forward.

Tang sprinted, pumping her arms at her sides. The air rushed in and out of her lungs. *Dee, Dee, Dee.* With heavy legs, she kicked up the sand. Passing Bert's moving body, she lunged toward the finish, her trail of footprints washed clean by the incoming tide.

Acknowledgments

I would like to thank Jovana Shirley for editing the manuscript.

Thanks to Robin Johnson for the inspiring artwork that encouraged me to finish this story.

Additional gratitude to Rose Turpin for educating me on the differences between romance, romantic suspense, and thrillers, and for her forgiveness for all those days during her childhood when I chose writing over playing with her.

Thanks to Nicole Zimmerman for discussing the manuscript with me. Her insight and questions spawned the dual narrative and provided for a more satisfying resolution.

As always, thanks to Kevin Gross for the time and space needed to write and his belief in my talents.

Finally, a shout out to all the people I interviewed about deception in personal relationships, both romantic and platonic. From sociopaths to catfishes to pathological liars, no matter what term was given to these deceptive individuals the feelings of shock, self-doubt, and disbelief remained in those whose trust had been betrayed. I honor your courage to share your stories of heartbreak and disillusionment. May you find peace and restored faith in humanity. Not everyone is full of darkness. Some people still have a spark of light.

Discussion Guide

1.   What did you think of Dee when you first met her? Were you surprised by her fabricated life? Do you agree with her decision to deceive Tang as well as her other lovers?

2.   Why does Tang connect with Dee so immediately? How is Tang different than Dee's other conquests? What do you think Tang sees in Dee? What do you think Dee sees in Tang?

3.   Tang has been with Layla for several years. How does Tang's relationship with Layla change throughout the novella?

4.   Were you surprised when you learned about what happened the night before the automobile accident? What version of events do you believe—Tang's or Dee's?

5.   Has there been a time in your life during which you told a lie that escalated beyond your control? Did you eventually tell the truth? Do you wish the events had played out differently?

6.   How does Dee change Tang? Discuss how her life is different at the end of the novella. Is Tang herself different?

7.   How is deception explored throughout the novella?

8.   Why does Layla choose to rebuild trust with Tang? Does Tang deserve a second chance?

9.   What role does family play throughout the novella? Have you ever been influenced by family in making major life decisions?

10.   Have you been involved in a deceptive relationship? Was it romantic or platonic? Discuss. What did you do when you discovered the truth? How does deception affect our society? Do you think this is different or changing in the age of social media?

11.   Were you surprised by how the novella ended? Why or why not?

About the Author

Angela Lam is a writing instructor with Gotham Writers' Workshop. She is the author of several contemporary romances, a short story collection, and two memoirs. *No Amends* is her debut suspense novella.

www.ingramcontent.com/pod-product-compliance
Lightning Source LLC
Chambersburg PA
CBHW050856180626
46814CB00007B/2773